# UTOPIA
# FIVE

## AE Currie

Anne Currie
@anne_e_currie
Visit my website at www.annecurrie.com

First Printing: Apr 2019

ISBN- 9781093609769

*To the team: Mum, Dad, Kath and the Jons*

*"Hello Lee.  I'm you"*

"The building circular—A cage, glazed—The prisoners in their cells, occupying the circumference—The officers in the centre. By blinds and other contrivances, the inspectors concealed [...] from the observation of the prisoners: hence the sentiment of a sort of omnipresence—The whole circuit reviewable with little, or if necessary without any, change of place. One station in the inspection part affording the most perfect view of every cell."

*Jeremy Bentham*
*Proposal for a New and Less Expensive mode of Employing and Reforming Convicts*
*(London, 1798)*

# CONTENTS

Prologue ...................................................................1

Rain ..........................................................................3

Panopticon...............................................................19

Explosions ...............................................................22

Reality ......................................................................27

Company ..................................................................31

Denizens ..................................................................47

Happiness.................................................................54

Corner ......................................................................70

Meltdown .................................................................80

God............................................................................85

Dystopia ...................................................................96

Host ...........................................................................99

Ergodicity................................................................108

Refugees...................................................................113

A Lift.........................................................................120

Zoom.........................................................................122

Time Travel .............................................................128

Judgement................................................................130

Nemo ........................................................................138

Dragons ...................................................................141

New Order................................................................145

Help ..........................................................................147

Enemy .......................................................................150

Execution .................................................................156

Crime........................................................................168

Free Will...................................................................173

Arrival ....................................................................181

Displaced ............................................................189

Angelsea..............................................................195

Guardians............................................................201

Control................................................................206

Hot Summer .......................................................211

Change ...............................................................216

Two Worlds..........................................................219

Utopia Five .........................................................226

The Castle............................................................229

Pivot ...................................................................239

Challenge.............................................................242

Escape .................................................................254

Trump Suit..........................................................260

Cheating ..............................................................270

Epilogue ..............................................................275

Timeline ..............................................................279

CHAPTER 1 – ARRIVAL ..........................................281

# PROLOGUE

## *Control 1963*

I'll never forget where I was the day President Kennedy was shot. I was standing on a grassy knoll in downtown Dallas with the sun blazing down and a piece of lead piping in my hand

"You know that's against the rules," said my brother Nemo who was standing beside me. "No changes before 2025. We don't have the data. Anyway, this is a cut scene. You can thump the shooter as hard as you like, it won't make a difference."

I grinned, "I know. Maybe I just wanted this for my autobiography."

"A bit hackneyed?" said Nemo.

## *Analog 2053*

My name is Lee Sands, and I was born on the 8th of January 2025. The day the Panopticon was turned on.

# RAIN

*Utopia Five 2053*

In grey freezing drizzle, I materialized in front of Big Ben. Even in a Utopia it rained occasionally, but this world seemed relentlessly wet. Did it have a sky? Or had Nemo not bothered?

I pelted inside the nearest pub, shivering, annoyed, and deciding I was an idiot for not appearing indoors in the first place. Cold water trickled down the inside of my collar and I grimaced. Why on earth did my suit emulate a damp neck? You could clearly take virtual reality too far. My hulking avatar was dressed in a noir-style trench coat, which was artfully unbuttoned. As a result, it wasn't a great deal of use. I caught a glimpse of myself in one of the interior's dark mirrors. I looked soggy.

This would be my ninth trip to this sim, and I hadn't spotted a single thing that was good about it yet, never mind utopian. I was starting to question why I'd let Nemo pivot this world. How was this murky version of the planet something to aspire to? Whatever the clever reason, that kind of subtlety was not part of our brand. To be honest, it wasn't usually part of Nemo's either.

I walked up to the bar and ordered a drink. On the wall a TV was playing at low volume. The screen showed a pink chat show host interviewing a mahogany-tanned celebrity. It was a distracting contrast to my otherwise colourless surroundings. I guessed they'd be discussing entertainment gossip. Utopia Five appeared to have an endless desire for it. I'd already worked out this was a standard capitalist society. No free beer but plenty of free speech. Of a sort.

The barman was a greasy-looking guy who was holding a grimy cloth and appeared to be miserable about both those facts. For a Utopia, this world had plenty of shit jobs. Undeterred by his gloomy demeanour, my avatar gave him a (literally) patented winning smile. "Busy day?"

He merely grunted. "The name's Eloi," I continued cheerfully and put out my hand.

While he stared in slight bewilderment at my friendly gesture, I pondered his attractiveness. It was unusually low for one of our worlds. A sim denizen being less than Brad Pitt in the looks department told me quite a lot about his real-life counterpart. As all VR programmers knew, in an emulation everyone had to be a lot better looking than they were in reality. We humans liked to kid ourselves. Everyone's virtual versions were heavily airbrushed. Otherwise, they wouldn't play.

Unfortunately, by Dystopia Two Nemo and I had also reluctantly realised our games needed some normal-looking denizens, or the world wasn't convincing. We couldn't add any extra characters so some of our emulated folks would have to forego their looks upgrade. It was sad but necessary.

We knew the human counterparts of those unairbrushed inhabitants would never visit, because who wanted to be in a world where everyone was great-looking apart from the local version of you? It would be demoralizing and probably embarrassing. You'd need a Teflon-coated ego or a personality disorder.

We ended up writing an algorithm to identify the real-worlders we were going to sacrifice to verisimilitude. They were usually poor, dull, and lacking in prospects. We wouldn't miss them as players, and they were low value to our sponsors. Those selected denizens stayed looking exactly as they did in life.

If you come into one of our emulations and the sim version of you looks like the real you, I hate to break it to you, you're either exceptionally attractive already or a loser. I leave that to you to decide. I had drawn my own conclusions about the man in front of me.

The bartender eventually shook my outstretched hand. That gained me his attention and a frisson of goodwill. I'd need it.

"Weather's pretty awful. Must be affecting business?" I glanced at the almost empty bar. A lone family in baseball caps were huddled around mugs of hot product placement opportunity. I mentally winced. We'd never sell these slightly depressed locations to our usual sponsors. Unless a mutant was about to burst through the door and slaughter everyone with a machine gun? I looked around hopefully. The only action was an ad break on the TV.

The barman shrugged. "When isn't it?"

He handed me my requested beer along with a handful of change. I placed my pint on a mat advertising umbrellas and pocketed the cash.

"The Government, eh?" I usually found bland comments to be useful for eliciting information from the locals without giving away I knew nothing at all about the world. Of course, Utopia Five might have been an ungoverned anarchy but I could usually spot those. No beer mats for a start.

The barman nodded in vigorous agreement with my content-free statement. "Yeah, bunch of crooks. All in it for themselves."

I sighed. I'd noticed this world of Nemo's seemed populated with opinionated but uninformed denizens. No wonder this character was wiping down tables. I wondered what his alter ego did in real life.

My avatar raised its cloudy beer and took a large, demoralised gulp. I'd learned surprisingly little in this so-called Utopia by wandering around questioning simulated inhabitants. Since my first visit, I'd realised the newspapers and TV stations were entirely filled with bland celebrity tittle-tattle. They weren't going to tell me much either. I swirled my pint.  I needed a starting point, and I was fast running out of my usual options.

My job in Utopia Five was the same as any player's.  I had to figure out how Nemo had changed the past to create the world I was now in. In half our games it was me who altered time.  For this sim, the world builder was my little brother.  It was my role to test it out and decide if it was worth pouring marketing money into and releasing as the next blockbuster from Nautilus Games.

Was it ready for our army of loyal players? Or only fit to be dumped in the virtual trash bin?  I knew what I was currently thinking.

My plan had been to play the world through, do some investigating, and discover the pivot Nemo had used to divert the course of history.  Easy.  Or so I'd thought. As my avatar, I could do anything in the game a real detective could.  Oh, plus instantly transport myself in space and time and change my appearance.  I could also gradually make myself invisible by turning down my opacity from one hundred percent to zero.  You'd be surprised how handy all that was. Apart from the fading in and out. That was completely pointless. I just liked it.

I'd started as I usually did in a new world: by visiting landmarks. Nemo preferred something iconic to get blown up in a pivot. He believed there was nothing more poignant than the smoldering ruin of a famous building, and he didn't think a metaphor could ever be too heavy-handed. I'd played all his games and was forced to agree. I'd also discovered a jagged Eiffel Tower, or a toppled Statue of Liberty was an excellent conversation starter. It made a great place to begin tracking down exactly where history had gone off the rails.

To my irritation, I'd found everything in this world to be frustratingly intact.

My avatar frowned at the lacklustre bartender and looked around the dingy pub again. The silent family were staring at the TV screen and out of the window, through the rain, I could see the disappointingly whole Big Ben. I suddenly realised I didn't want to play this damp and depressing game any longer. It was time to do something I normally avoided.  I needed to take a long hard look at myself.

One of the ways Nautilus VR was different from the real world was players didn't have an all-seeing, all-knowing presence they could get advice from.  Nemo and I deliberately hadn't installed a deity in any of our sims.  After all, God was a well-known spoilsport and would definitely have given the game away.  To be honest, we also couldn't afford the license fees.  We already handed a fortune over to Omniscience Industries for Panopticon data and we didn't have the money for anything else.  The divine word wasn't cheap.

Fortunately, for me, talking to the local copy of Lee Sands usually had the same effect and was considerably more affordable.  No version of me would ever fail to provide a free opinion, at length, on the state of world affairs and how we got there. I knew how to push my own buttons.  I also knew talking to my own denizen to get the lowdown on a sim world was kind of cheating.  What the hell. Nemo didn't need to find out.

Before I spilled all, however, I decided to try one final trick. My next destination would be the North London flat in 2043 where Nemo and I had lived back then. If everything was exactly as I remembered in '43 I'd jump forward to 2048, halfway between 2043 and now. If it was still identical, I'd jaunt to 2051. I could hop about like that until I'd worked out where history started to diverge. In my opinion, that wasn't cheating, and it wouldn't take long. I was entering my first jump into the player interface when my sixth sense kicked in. A faint tingling in my spine told me someone in the seemingly empty pub was watching me.

If I accepted it for publishing, Utopia Five would be our 56th commercially available simulated world. It didn't matter if it was a Utopia or a Dystopia; the Nautilus promise was the biggest change from the smallest pivot. As soon as you stepped into one of our sims it was always clear how that world differed from ours back in reality. Giant dinosaurs fighting in the streets; a takeover by a bloodsucking zombie elite; a talking dog for World President. 'Go big or go home' was the

Nautilus credo and our legion of fans clearly agreed.

When Nemo or I were building a new sim, first we'd decide what we wanted. Let's say a cure for age. Then we'd work out who we would've had to persuade, pay, or assassinate in our own world's past to get it. That usually took a few months of research. We had a few tricks to help us out. Of course, we didn't know what would've really happened if we'd changed the past. Our new world was just guaranteed to be 100% possible.

Our speculative fiction algorithm extrapolated out from the pivot. Once we'd changed things, we ran the recalculations, rippled the consequences through to the present time, and that was our sim. Sometimes it was a Utopia. Mostly it wasn't. If it was cool enough, we released it. "Age is Cured!" was Dystopia Nineteen. It was one of our biggest hits. Everyone loves a horror.

I'd been struggling to build Utopia Five for a while. My past Utopian worlds had been modest successes: an ecology hit, a cool solar system exploration sim, and then I finally got superpowers working. I'd even had a surprise cult hit with "Utopia Four: Talk to the Animals!" That was a bit of an accidental find. The problem was, Utopias were hard to generate at all, never mind with a small change. Dystopias were easy. They also got a bit depressing after you'd done twenty in a row, even if they did sell well. I was struggling to work out what I wanted for my next Utopia when Nemo told me he'd had an idea. Six months later, he announced Utopia Five was ready to launch and I just needed to test it out. He'd even created me a new avatar: Eloi.

The trouble was, for a game to be successful the difference between it and our world had to be bleeding obvious. How a sim world differed from the real one wasn't the puzzle. It was the hook. If we didn't grab players inside 30 seconds, we'd lost them. They needed a spectacular or at least intriguing idea to suck them in. I'd been playing Utopia Five for nearly fifty hours and, apart from the bad weather, I hadn't worked out how it was significantly different to analog reality yet. I couldn't see what Nemo was getting at. Half a year of investment and this world wasn't going to be a hit. What the hell was he thinking? Nevertheless, I could hardly let him win. I'd solve Utopia Five if it killed me.

When I talked about my "sixth sense" it wasn't a figure of speech. Nemo wouldn't let me give my avatars any special powers. "In the game, every player is equal," he used to say sanctimoniously and fairly frequently, and I never broke the rules. I merely coded up a lot of publicly available avatar features. Anyone could install them if they wanted.

In release 34.762.08 I added a brand new ability. It was on general release. Not even premium. 'Ear Wiggle 0.1' allowed any avatar to agitate their lobes on demand. Oh, and feel the presence of other players in their vicinity with zero opacity. Well, if people didn't read the documentation all the way to the end that wasn't my fault. I was apparently the only player who'd turned on the feature.

It wasn't unusual for me to detect invisible avatars in my prox. I was well known. Lots of players followed me around hoping to pick up clues about pivots. That could have worked, which was why I'd snuck my sixth sense, masquerading as a frivolous customisation, into the games platform. I wanted to be able to avoid tipping anyone off about a change I was researching. With my faux-supernatural power enabled, I was used to getting notifications about hidden onlookers in the other worlds. In Utopia Five, however, I was supposed to be the only person with a login other than Nemo. Who was watching me?

## Analog 2053

Disturbed by my mysterious observer, I flipped up my visor and exited the game. That left me standing in a dark neoprene-looking suit, staring at the inside of the small flat I had been about to visit in the fictional past of an alternative world. If that was confusing, I was more than used to it.

The real-world room around me was empty as usual and featureless save for a huge photo-array of world leaders in politics, business, science and the arts. I frowned. They were due for their annual refresh. Then I wrinkled my nose and sniffed. Something wasn't right.

Now my mask was raised, I could clearly detect the room was full of what smelled strongly like gas. I glanced briefly at the door, 20 feet away, and leapt straight out of the open window next to me. My suit could handle a fifteen-foot fall. A close quarter's explosion was outside the specs.

I dropped unexpectedly out of the sky onto the road in front of my house. As I thumped to the ground, it passed through my mind it would be ironic to escape being blown to smithereens in my own lounge only to get knocked over by a passing car. The odds, however, were good. Hardly anyone drove anymore. I landed with just a touch of servo-assist, started sprinting and looked around at the empty street. That was good. If an…

"Woof!!"

I had no time to finish my thought.

My suit wasn't the best money could buy. It was way better than that. Nemo liked to spend his earnings on real estate. I always thought, "What's the point of money if you can't take it with you?" Plus, I preferred my consumption to be less conspicuous. And less kitsch if we're being brutally honest about Nemo's home decor choices.

A wall of force pushed my suit forward hard. I went with it and we kept a running grip on the tarmac. The visor had snapped down in the jump and the proximity detector gave us plenty of time to dodge the larger chunks of descending masonry. Did I anthropomorphize the suit much? Shh. You'll hurt its feelings.

After a few seconds, the scanners gave me the all-clear on falling debris. I stopped running and turned back to the charred ruins of the tenement that had been my home for over a decade. I sighed. *Damn.*

If I seemed unconcerned about my apartment neighbours it was because they were servers. That wasn't a euphemism for people who walked around in high heels on laminate floors and whom I would be glad to see as smoldering piles of charcoal. No, Nemo and I had solved that particular problem in '45 when we bought the place out and turned it over to test systems. My fellow residents in that building were all machines. The only human in the vicinity had been me.

A gas explosion. It was a classic accident. They happened. Except, I wasn't on gas. The whole country had stopped using it in the '40s. I scowled. A gas canister was relatively easy to turn into a makeshift bomb with a remote trigger. We'd all done that.

Like most people, I never locked my apartment. Why would I? No one robbed anyone anymore. You'd trivially get caught and what was worth stealing? I thought about my spare room, which I hardly used. I was pretty sure I hadn't been in there since Nemo last stayed and that was months ago. On consideration, someone could have walked right in and hidden anything they wanted. I wouldn't spot it for weeks.

The odour of gas might be obvious, but I hadn't smelt anything with my visor down. If someone ensured I was in a game before they triggered the gas, they could have converted me into ten thousand tiny pieces before I'd even noticed. If my mysterious watcher hadn't freaked me out in Utopia Five, right at that moment I would be gently coating London in a light layer of ash. But why on earth would anyone want me dead?

# PANOPTICON

## *Analog 2025*

In the early 2020's, the British public finally started to grumble about how much they were being observed.  From our modern perspective it seems astonishing it took so long.  For years, they had been, perhaps, the most watched populace in history.   Private companies and their own government videoed them whenever they went in public and listened to them in private.

After the drug legalisation of 2022, organised crime moved into big data.   With all that surveillance material, blackmail was big business. Half the country was trying to keep their secrets secret.  The other half were inexorably working out what they were up to.  All of it was a colossal waste of human effort.

Eventually, a bright politician decided to sell British voters on a radically new proposition.  We should either stop the observation or stop the secrecy. We had learned from the war on drugs and chose the second option. We took down our figurative net curtains and embraced exposure. On Transparency Day in January 2025, all the data feeds from the UK's huge drone observation fleet and from cameras and microphones across the kingdom went open to everyone. From then on, every recording device used in public anywhere in the country had to be licensed and make its data available to all. The Brits called it The Panopticon.

The theory was, everyone should be able to see and hear everything. There would be no more secrets and we'd have to judge or accept people as they were. In reality, it wasn't quite that straightforward.

The first problem was coverage. The recordings were incredibly patchy. Central London was awash with cameras and mics, everywhere else was a lot less monitored. Private buildings were a complete dead zone. Second, there was too much information. We suddenly had tens of millions of 24/7 video feeds and we didn't have the computational power to do anything with them. It became like the old public cameras in the British Houses of Parliament - nice in theory, but who could be bothered watching? We had no clue what we were going to do with all the footage. Eventually, we learned one man did have an idea.

After the Panopticon went live, an unknown British programmer called Kirby Cross decided to use his gossipy chatbot as an interface into the data. You could ask it any question and his bot would answer as best it could by searching the Panopticon feeds. It took him five years to get working. Version one of the chatbot from Cross' Omniscience Industries went live in April 2030.

No-one could have predicted what Deus would become.

# EXPLOSIONS

## *Analog 2053*

Someone was trying to kill me.  I needed to find out who that was, and I urgently needed to hand the information over to the police.  My skintight suit shouldn't fool anyone - I was a computer programmer not a vigilante.

17 seconds after the explosion, I was standing on my street gazing at the toppled remains of my home when I heard sirens and saw the first wave of a thousand approaching drones.  The large-scale aerial response time round here was less than 30 seconds and the arriving quadcopters immediately began extinguishing flames around the pulverized remains of my building.  I switched to the Panopticon bird's eye view and enabled infrared. The fires were already mostly out and there were no signs of any injured bystanders.  Excellent, but

unsurprising. By 2053, we were spectacularly good at firefighting and we knew how to manage a crisis.

Within the next minute, an event marked 'Bell St. Explosion 15022053' had been created in the city's network and a management team assigned. I watched residents begin to emerge from houses with buckets, brooms, and spades and start registering clean-up efforts in the drone-identified safe zones. Orders for equipment delivery were being fired at the North London Distribution Centre. I waved at a camera and the system logged I was alive, accounted for, and seemingly unharmed. Everything appeared to be under control.

I looked across at the terrace of previously spotless houses on the other side of my road. A woman was standing in an open doorway at the end of the street, pulling on her coat. She glared out at what was left of the buildings opposite and I saw the event handling system accept her request for prime status. She was in charge now. To be assigned direction, she might be a retired teacher, a professional engineer, or just a highly trusted civilian with logged organisational experience. I happened to know she ran the local library. I pulled back my hood and walked towards her.

"Lee!" she shouted. "I've volunteered to run clean-up and investigation on your event. I've never done an explosion before! It should be interesting." She looked concerned for a moment. "Are you alright? I assume you just arrived?"

Mrs Lewis was noted for her unflappable composure. Not wishing to be outdone, I informed her I had been inside the house until the explosion and the cause was probably a gas canister, which may have been hidden in my spare room. "I intend to track down the culprit." I shook my head. "I apologise for the mess."

"Oh Lee! Thank you for that report. It was very..." she paused. "Calm, under the circumstances."

She took her glasses out of her handbag and put them on her nose. "I'm glad you're okay but do remember we follow the rule of law in London. We have a professional police force. Tracking down criminals is what we pay them for." She gave me a hard look. "You don't need to do it yourself. This isn't Colchester." She looked for a moment as if she wanted to pat me on the head, checked herself and frowned. "Go and get a nice cup of tea and a biscuit. That's an order. We'll handle things. And don't worry about the mess. Worse things happen at sea."

She was right. These days, some pretty eye-watering stuff happened at sea. I didn't see how that was relevant.

Having ascertained Mrs Lewis and her friends had the situation under control, I reckoned I could afford to take off and do some investigation of my own before the trail got cold. I jogged to the community kitchen two streets over where I normally ate. I was a little dusty but otherwise uninjured. Nothing a hot drink wouldn't fix. I walked inside the cafeteria, poured myself a mug of the prescribed tea, and peered into the biscuit tin. I decided rich teas were not up to consoling me for the loss of my home and all my worldly goods, never mind the revelation that someone was trying to kill me. I opened a cupboard and looked around for the custard creams.

*That explosion was a close call*, I thought. I was rather impressed at myself for keeping so cool during my first analog assassination attempt. It happened all the time in VR, but the real world was normally a lot more law abiding. Nothing that exciting had happened to me since the Hot Summer.

I wolfed down a biscuit while musing that under the circumstances I had probably deserved a chocolate-covered digestive. Unfortunately, those were a rare treat in this kitchen. Perhaps I should be contributing more to local resources? I decided I needed to look into that. Right at that moment, however, I didn't have time to ponder the economics of cooperative food allocation. I needed to log into Control, identify my would-be assassin, and have them arrested ASAP. Control was our flagship product. A 100% live-synchronized world emulator with full archive and replay functionality. It was where I'd find what I wanted to know. No one could hide from Lee Sands there. I smiled in anticipation. From now on, I was the one in control.

I stood up, primed my suit, and issued the verbal launch command, "Control. Authorization: Lee Sands. Location: here. Time: now!"

Nothing happened.

# REALITY

*Analog 2039*

Nemo and I built Control first. Of course, it wasn't called that to start with. Back then, it was just another sim and there were thousands of those.

You probably know virtual reality finally got perfected in the 2040s. Personally, I was desperate for it by then. I guess most people were. After the hydrocarbon ban, a lot of humans found the analog world boring. Although, after '36 we knew things could be a lot worse than dull. Nemo and I were particularly aware of that, and we'd been lucky. During the Hot Summer we'd lived in the northern hemisphere.

There we were. Stuck in our dormitories. Bored out of our minds. Every spare adult was gardening, but kids had stopped being drafted for that in '39.

We were supposed to be concentrating on our lessons. The trouble was those was trivial. Nemo and I were on the lookout for something more interesting.

Virtual reality had been around for over a decade before the Hot Summer. Not everything had been destroyed and plenty of VR headsets, gloves, games servers, and solar panels were still knocking about. Kids like me and Nemo – the ones who had time on our hands – got very good at using that stuff. The internet was still powered for schoolwork and reference materials and Deus6 gave us access to just about every expert left on the planet. Nemo was unnaturally good at getting the chatbot to give him the information he wanted and the specialists it found for him were usually bored too. We had everything we needed.

It's amazing what you can achieve with a piece of kit if you're dying for some entertainment and you've absolutely nothing else to do. We all soon grokked mass production had gotten an order of magnitude more expensive and the global economy had tanked. No one was getting a hardware upgrade anytime soon. Software, however, we could change ourselves. So, we did.

Using the crappy kit we had left, we and the rest of the VR community took the existing basic VR to a believable immersive experience inside two years. Then, in 2041, WorldGov finally recognized an unentertained population was an unstable one and gave virtual reality access to public energy. Suddenly, we had power. VR eventually got reserved electricity user status alongside communications, education, and the Panopticon. We had tight limits, but we worked with them. It turned out humans were bloody good at solving problems when we didn't have a choice.

By 2042, the Panopticon was complete for most vaguely governed countries. Almost every home had at least one microphone and camera and everyone published their data. In London, Nemo and I reckoned anywhere you stood you were in viewing range of at least 1200 cameras. That turned out to be an underestimate. There was still no killer VR simulation for it all though and everyone was racing to build one. Including us.

Nemo and I had our eyes on the OmniscientView. Omniscience Industries' video data was vastly better than the free public stuff from the

Panopticon. Integrating all those millions of cameras was something only Omniscience had cracked. We needed that View, but it was way too expensive for a couple of obsessed schoolkids – or anyone short of a MegaCorp. Then Nemo spotted Kirby Cross' School Project Programme. It came with a free license. We put together a revoltingly saccharine plea to be included – we suspected that was required – and got a silver award.

Nemo was twelve. The license would cover us until he was sixteen and I learned a valuable lesson: you can never be too shameless in a grant application.

# COMPANY

## *Analog 2053*

Control was offline. So were Utopias One through Five. I even tried all the Dystopias. That took quite a while. Nothing was working. Staring around the canteen in desperation, I spotted a teenager playing games on a screen in the table in front of him and strode over. "Karl, can you log into the Nautilus platform right now?"

He took one look at my face and hurriedly brought up our welcome screen. Or didn't. "Sorry Lee, you're down."

Nearly getting blown up was one thing. Having our servers go offline appeared to be a whole new level of terror. My first thought was, *how could this happen? Our systems are state of the art!* My second was, *why the hell didn't I get alerted?*

We ran our stuff on the Omniscience cloud. If the live servers were unavailable, Omniscience should have turned my suit into a neon light show. Right now, I should come with an epilepsy warning. Except it hadn't happened. Could Omniscience be down?

"Karl!" I yelled, completely unnecessarily as he was four feet away. "Can you see Deus?"

"Yeah, it's fine. Everything is fine. It's just you."

Damn!

It took me 30 minutes of panicked denial, anger, bargaining with an Omniscience support team who were frustratingly well trained in social engineering attacks and would not let me in and, finally, misery to accept my Nautilus logins were disabled. The whole platform was dead, and I didn't have the authority to bring it back up. To ice that cake, the last-ditch emergency fallback systems were currently one hundred metres away in a charred heap.

My cunning plan to catch my bomb-wielding stalker would have to wait. I'd leave all that in the capable hands of Mrs. Lewis and her librarian assistants. I had bigger concerns.

The only person who could possibly have locked me out of Omniscience was my little brother. What the hell was he up to? The good news was, I wasn't completely cut off from the world. He could disable my Nautilus access, but he couldn't affect my personal accounts.

"Deus," I said, "Where's Nemo?"

God's voice spoke in my ear. "Exactly where he always is. He's at home. And he's refusing calls. If you want to talk to him, you'll have to travel there. You know what he's like."

I did know what my brother was like. I'd have to go. In the meantime, I left him a shouted voice message ordering him to log in and bring the systems back up. I had a suspicion it would have no effect. I balled my fists. It was nearly one hundred miles to Nemo's place. For the past year, he'd been living in a bizarre, isolated mansion on a particularly bleak patch of the English east coast. I could cycle there in around eight hours and it was so far off the beaten track there wasn't a faster option. I glanced at the time. There were only a few hours of daylight left.

It wasn't a great idea to use the roads at night. There were too many animals wandering around and I'd observed cows hardly ever wore high visibility jackets. They clearly had no sense of health and safety or, at least, no sense of my health and safety. Still, I should be able to get most of the way there before sunset and I could set off again at dawn. I'd be at Nemo's before he woke up.

My first problem was I had no money. I dashed back to Karl, who must be on a day off. "Could I borrow some cash?" I realised some explanation might be required. "My house just blew up."

"I noticed. Bummer." He started digging out notes from his pocket and handing them over. "Don't worry. I'll get it back from Mrs Lewis."

The bank of helpful neighbour turned out to be surprisingly well capitalized. Next, I ran into the kitchen and grabbed a large bag of flapjacks, some slightly wizened apples, and a thermos of tea. That should get me there. My suit was fully charged but I topped up the water from the cold tap.

In a stroke of luck, my ride had been in the shop for an upgrade that week. Otherwise, at that moment it would have been freewheeling in bicycle heaven, which would have made me particularly sad. I'd put a lot of effort into that bike. As it was, I could wave goodbye to Karl and sprint half a mile to where my transport should be waiting for me, oiled and ready to go. When I arrived, the proprietor, Sophie, gave me a tearful hug. Like everyone else in the vicinity she'd heard the blast and seen the videos. As she waved me off, she promised to keep an eye on my progress to Nemo's place.

Her concern reminded me that my dramatic escape and the plume of black smoke currently rising from North London had probably generated some interest on the Net. Inside my visor, I brought up my personal Panopticon dashboard and blinked. 1.789 million people were currently observing me through the public alert platforms. I had to assume one of them was my would-be assassin. *Unless he has an unusually short attention span,* I thought. However, knowing that wasn't much use to me. I couldn't look them all up and finding the only observer who mattered would be like finding a needle in a haystack. I frowned, then checked a name. Nemo wasn't watching.

My brother's hideout was exactly 93.7 miles north-east by road, and it was getting late.  I reckoned I could only cover 50 miles before it got dark and no matter how urgent this crisis was, I wasn't about to cycle in the pitch black with who-knows-what on the road in front of me.  I had some sophisticated IR scanners built into my suit, but I didn't want to shout about that, especially to nearly two million watching eyes, including a recently foiled assassin.  I'd have to camp out overnight.  Time to get moving.

I travelled up the slow lane of the motorway, weaving around creaking bikes pulling trailers; horse riders; ponies with traps; and copious potholes.  Self-driving trucks and busses whistled by in the automation lane.  I overtook two middle-aged women walking behind a pair of picturesque, yoked oxen and gave them a wave.  They looked startled to get 500,000 thumbs up from the people who were still watching me, presumably in the hope something else would blow up.

The generally agreed road speed limit was 20 miles-an-hour in the two slow lanes.  People walking, stationary livestock, and gaping holes were common though. You had to pay attention.

The speeding electric behemoths were limited to the carefully maintained outside lane. Thank Deus, they never ventured into our more dilapidated zone to overtake one another because they never overtook one another. And to join the hurtling train, each vehicle waited patiently for a gap long enough for them to get up to speed. To be honest, not much of a break was required. I always thought their acceleration was uncanny, even though I'd seen it a hundred times. It made the real world feel like a sim. I quite liked that.

Every time I took the bike out, I enjoyed the juxtaposition of the very human lanes and the completely inhuman outer one. I found the folk in the organic zones were generally friendly. The best thing about 2053 was the people were pretty relaxed. Mostly because everyone was busy, and no one was starving. Tired? Frequently. Desperate, hungry, or destitute? Never. World President Gates saw to that. He was a believer in order and, love him or hate him, he usually delivered. I'd assassinated him twice and both times it was a mistake.

Our only problem in '53 was energy. Fusion was still twenty years off and I was beginning to get a teeny bit sceptical about the whole thing. Power cramped my style in every world. Most of our competitor sims had at least got jet cars, but I could never make the economics work outside of a Dystopia.

I'd wanted to pivot one of our worlds for some cool new form of energy and I even had ideas for how to do it. It would have been great. The problem was, Nemo wouldn't let a pivot change the laws of physics. He reckoned that was cheating. He was always a spoilsport. Not that that would have helped me with this journey, anyway. It had all the tedious limitations of reality.

After about three hours of riding, it began to get dark and the humans on the road started to thin out. Unlike the organic drivers, the autonomous traffic would continue in its high–speed stream all night. The cows steered clear of it. Perhaps I had underestimated their grasp of health and safety.

Deus informed me there were a couple of houses within a mile of my location with a spare bed for the night and I thought wistfully about mattresses. However, with an explosion in my recent history; several hundred thousand observers waiting for the next one; and presumably a frustrated murderer on my tail; I felt I wasn't an ideal houseguest. I would be sleeping outside.

With my actual eyes, I could see a small camp in a layby ahead. A range of interesting tents, a covered cart, and plenty of humans and animals wandering about. I even saw two shire horses looming on the grass verge. I could sleep literally anywhere in my suit, but this setup would provide people to talk to. I didn't check their reputations with Deus. What the hell, they were randomly chosen. Unlikely to contain the mysterious mortal enemy I seemed to have acquired.

I pulled in and got off my bike. It was synced with my suit so it wouldn't move anywhere if I wasn't on it. Any attempt to lift it more than a few feet would provide an extremely attractive strobing display for everyone in the vicinity. I took off my helmet, visor, and hood then ruffled my buzz cut. Hood hair was such a pain. I would have liked to just shave my head completely. I found folk tended to see that as weird, when in my opinion it was merely sensible.

I walked over to the group, most of whom were sitting around a glowing object. For some reason, a flickering campfire no longer engendered the comforting feelings it once had. These days, we were happy to get our warm fuzzies encircling a battery-powered camping torch.

I hoped to buy my way into the group with friendly charm and some flapjacks. I had a bottle of decent whisky in my rucksack. I decided not to flash it around yet. It marked me out as having money, which was risky given that right now I didn't. Crime was almost unheard of, but there was no point asking for it.

"Hi, I'm Lee", I said with my usual in-game grin. "You look comfortable. May I join you? I bring snacks courtesy of my excellent local kitchen."

Oddly, I didn't feel the tingling alert that would signal someone close by had checked my ID or reputation score. The motley folk just waved me in and shuffled to create a gap, with apparently no qualms. I didn't feel worried about them myself; they were predominantly women and kids and mostly smiling. Though, as a wise man once said, one may smile and smile and be a villain. I sat on the ground. Fortunately, it was dry. I really hated taking the suit into mud.

"How do you do Lee," said a very old woman separated from me by two wrestling children and a large pile of sewing that appeared to belong to her. "My name is Laura. Laura Close. Where are you going to so fast on that lovely-looking bicycle?"

In the real world there was no point being less than truthful or economical with the facts. They were easy to check if you could be bothered. "I'm heading to see my brother. Our VR system is mysteriously offline, and he is the only person left with a login." I paused. "Oh, and someone is trying to kill me but Mrs. Lewis is currently handling that." I felt that covered all the key information. "I should get to Nemo's tomorrow. I didn't want to cycle in the dark."

"How sensible of you," came a voice from a dimly lit man on the other side of the circle, who mysteriously appeared to already be chewing on one of my flapjacks. I glanced suspiciously at the box in my hand. "Very good," he said. "I congratulate your chef. My name is Mr. Creek and I respect a person who is willing to put their life in the hands of a librarian. Welcome to our travelling band."

You may have noticed this whole encounter had rapidly gone a bit Brothers Grimm. I always enjoyed a game. Clearly, once I'd entered the circle the rule was no more accessing the net. I glanced casually about me. Laura Close and Mr. Creek were not really in the Nautilus demographic. Next to the old lady was a teenage boy staring at me with his mouth open. I threw a flapjack over to him. "What's your favourite?"

"Dystopia Fifteen!" He yelled as he grabbed the flying snack. Then he went bright red and looked sheepish.

Mr. Creek laughed. "Indeed, Sandy recognized you as soon as you took your hood off. He's rather a fan, so we looked you up. You've had an eventful day. Call me Ray and let me introduce you to the rest of my companions. You already know Laura and Sandy." We nodded. "Meet Sixpenny and Tenpenny." They proved to be the two children who were quietly attempting to strangle one another. "And their father Stone." I dipped my head to a fair man in his mid-forties. Sixpenny and Tenpenny remained engrossed in their current pursuits. "And finally, meet Catterwade."

The last member of the party was a rather saturnine woman probably ten years older than me and the only other person wearing a suit. We gave one another guarded smiles. Ray Creek turned out to be cheerfully loquacious, stocky, slightly grizzled and in his late fifties, at my guess. He seemed delighted to tell me all about the small company gathered around the light.

The Panopticon had destroyed and created many occupations in the past 28 years, and it appeared this group exemplified those changes. Laura and Ray were line walkers and most of the younger folk were drone seekers. Ray informed me that in the 2020s he had been "in crime". I wasn't sure if he meant he was a policeman or a criminal and it seemed rude to ask. Whichever the starting point the ultimate results were the same. Both professions had effectively disappeared. My recent problems aside, the police force we still had in London were mostly social workers. The vast majority of 999 calls these days involved someone who'd lost their login details. Crime was hardly worth it when all the victim or investigator usually had to do was ask Deus who did it. Ray's departure from the criminal activity business was therefore a common story. Laura's tale was more interesting.

One of the agreed responsibilities of the city states was food & shelter for every inhabitant. WorldGov contributed and the whole thing was monitored by the Panopticon. The system worked reasonably well, and most cities complied. It helped WorldGov's tax collection that the old tax avoidance states had gone. They hadn't put much effort into protecting their populace from the Summer and there weren't many people keen on helping them rebuild, particularly as they'd never joined the Panopticon. Since '36, we've had little idea what's been going on in those old, haven islands. We just leave them out of the sims. I'd always been surprised so many people put their money into such fragile states. I guess folk really did fetishize secrecy in the olden days. Ray proudly told us that Laura had been involved in all that somehow, working for a very important international organisation that was long gone. Laura remained discreetly silent on the subject.

I thought about Laura's old job. There had always been the risk that free food and housing would mean everyone lounged about like lotus-eaters in a fashion historically disapproved of by Captain Kirk and other authoritarian personality-types. It didn't work out that way. The minimum rations were perfectly fine but rather dull. Everyone found jobs to do that appealed to them and brought in extra cash and variety. We all muddled along. Line walkers were one of those niche occupations. These days, Ray and Laura walked the power lines doing inspections and small-scale maintenance, slowly travelling the land by horse and wagon. They didn't handle emergencies, just the regular, manual routine that makes emergencies less common and keeps everything ticking over. If they spotted a bigger problem, they alerted the powered teams. The pair synched up with other walkers via the Net and the Panopticon paid them all for their services.

Ray described how, in the middle of the last decade, he and Laura had picked up Stone and the kids along the way. Then they'd all run into Catterwade, a seeker. She was wandering the countryside finding and fixing downed drones to sell back to the Panopticon. As it turned out, the children were pretty good at finding and the line walkers trails went through prime drone-hunting territory.

Catterwade joined the group. Now Stone and Sandy helped her fix whatever broken devices she found. They kept some of what they restored to build up their own small drone fleet, which helped them search a wider area. The group worked well together.

"There is always something lost to find or fix, and we all enjoy the work," said Ray. "It's part of keeping society functioning.  There are still plenty of jobs that need humans."

Laura, who had been quietly listening to Ray's long description of their lives suddenly asked me a question about my own. "So, Sandy tells me you re-imagine the world for a living?"

I was always happy to talk about the games, so I started to explain the basic concept of how Nautilus made the Utopias and Dystopias.

"We create alternate worlds.  Imagine a small change happened in the past and that change rippled forward to create a different present," I said. "Sometimes it's better: a Utopia, sometimes it's worse: a Dystopia.  That's our game.  The players investigate the new world, travel into its past, and work out what the change was.  It's a lot of fun." Sandy nodded vigorously. "The only problem," I continued, "is mostly when we make our change the alternative world isn't that exciting. The differences can be pretty subtle.  Those worlds we delete.  Some worlds turn out really interesting though and we publish them."

Sandy looked shocked.  "But what about all the people in those other worlds! Are you saying you just kill them?"

# DENIZENS

*Analog 2040*

Winning the Omniscience school prize had gotten us four years of free access to the OmniscientView.  It wasn't as sophisticated back then as it is now, but it still kicked the backside of all the other Panopticon data feeds and having it gave us a huge advantage over everyone else in VR. Everyone apart from the MegaCorps, of course. They just paid up and bought the View, but the Megas were full of boring old people.  We had a big advantage over anyone who mattered.  Anyone who was going to do anything interesting.

We also had time.  School was easy, so we spent almost every waking moment writing code.  Nemo and I released our first VR simulation in 2042. Nautilus 1.0.  We called it 'Sauron's Eye' and it was the first shit hot full-world emulator based on Panopticon data.  Eventually, it would become

Control. Back in '42 we thought Sauron was our killer product. That didn't last long.

Sauron's Eye was amazing. You could time travel back to look at any event since the Panopticon was switched on: the day I was born in 2025. The early years could be a bit flaky. The data was thin back then. Let's be honest though, it was a superpower. Unfortunately, when we released it to the world it turned out there was a problem.

In '42, the OmniscientView feeds were not real-time. All that merging together of billions of cameras across the globe? Well, it turns out that takes time. Who'd have guessed? We hadn't worried about that for Sauron; it was so obvious we didn't think about the product impact. Anyone could already see targeted single feeds directly from the Panopticon with no delay because they were raw. It was processing and merging the feeds together that gave you virtual reality rather than just a bunch of videos. That wasn't free or quick. It took Omniscience minutes, or even days, to do it. The OmniscientView trailed behind reality.

Every Sauron's Eye user complained. With nearly 30 years of history to explore, most people just wanted to look at what was going on next door right at that moment. When the moment passed so, apparently, did their interest. Our tests showed most of humanity had a maximum attention span of 12.8 minutes. The average Sauron's Eye reality lag was 13.7 minutes. We bombed.

It was Nemo's 14th birthday and we had two years left on the license.

## Analog 2042

So, what could we do with what we had? We decided to add some gameplay. By then, the whole VR community had realized we could cheaply convert our stillsuits to haptics and feel our sims as well as see them. Our immersive experiences got a whole lot more tactile. Nemo added touch into Nautilus fairly easily, but we knew it wouldn't be enough to sell Sauron's Eye. In fact, it made things worse. Being able to touch made it even more frustrating you were only a watcher. You couldn't interact with the people you were seeing. Could we fix that?

We started working on behavioural prediction algorithms. There was a load of prior art already out there on behaviour. We needed to tie it together with what we had, which was a shitload of video and audio data.

For any individual, at any time covered by the Panopticon feeds (other than the last 15 minutes, of course) we had data on everything they had ever done or said in response to the stimuli they had encountered. We knew their facial expressions and body postures before they had taken those actions.

We could generate behavioural models for everyone and we had detailed information about what they actually did next to test those models against. That was everything we needed.

Denizens. That's what we called our simulated humans. In any given scenario, our Nautilus Behavioural Predictor made educated guesses for a denizen's next action. It then judged its algorithm against what the Panopticon showed actually happened next and improved it.

In theory, every real human had a denizen equivalent and every one of them got their own algorithm. In reality, we found most people weren't that different. We could use 41 basic behavioural models with 102 variants to cover every human fairly accurately. The model and variants changed over time for each individual.

At any point, Nautilus reckoned we only needed 4,000 different kinds of person to produce a complex world that approximated closely enough to the real one. Of course, there was also some behavioural randomness. Some individuals were more predictable than others.

We needed to keep one sim world close to the real, analog one. That was where we generated and assigned all the individual behaviour models. We already used the Panopticon feeds to keep Nautilus 1, Sauron's Eye, as close to Analog as possible. We used that and renamed it Control.

We launched Nautilus 2.0 in 2043. Nemo called it "The Time Machine". It was fantastic. Our players could have convincing, realistic conversations with anyone in history. Well, anyone since 2025. Not ancient history. Unfortunately, there was a problem.

The thing about highly realistic human interactions is that, realistically, most famous people from history will not have sex with you. Apparently, that came as an unpleasant surprise to most of our players. We bombed.

It was 8 months to Nemo's 16th birthday.

## Analog 2043

We had one last shot.

Could we use the Nautilus engine to predict the future and pay the OmniscientView license fees with betting? We could definitely use Nautilus to predict *a* future: in one place, for one person, for a very short time. For that it was great. In limited scenarios, we could reduce the possible futures down to a few hundred possibilities. Maybe a thousand. But *the* future? What even was that? It only existed in retrospect. For the kind of future you could bet on and win, Nautilus was a disaster. There were too many variables. Sports were a particular nightmare. Football was 92.7% random chance. We had written a speculative fiction engine not an oracle. Nautilus showed you a future that might well happen. It seldom actually did. Gambling was not going to save us.

When we did finally hit the jackpot, it was a complete fluke.

By the middle of '43, things were getting fraught. We were nearly out of road on our license and Nemo and I were bickering constantly over anything and everything. Late one night, he and I were having one of our regular heated arguments about World President Gates. I was contending the world would have done just as well without Gates, maybe he'd even held us back. Nemo didn't agree. I got so angry I went back to 2025 in Control, shot Gates, forked my world and rolled it forward to 2043.

Do you remember that 'flu crisis in 2034? The Nautilus engine thought it could have ended very differently without the inoculation program. While we were still struggling with a global pandemic, we wouldn't have been able to organize fast enough to handle the Hot Summer. In fact, according to the predictions of Nautilus, with no Gates the Summer would have triggered a complete civilization collapse. The US would have been an anarchic free-for-all by 2043. Europe would have been mostly comprised of feudal dictators re-running the 100 years' war with Kalashnikovs. It was really cool.

I paid up the chocolate bar I owed Nemo and published our sim as the first Nautilus Games title: "Dystopia One: Global Meltdown!"

It was the VR game of the year.

# HAPPINESS

## *Analog 2053*

Sandy was looking at me as if I'd killed someone. Actually, he thought I'd killed several hundred billion people. He just hadn't realised that yet. I'd often noticed his current expression didn't scale anyway. People looked equally horrified whether they momentarily believed I've killed one person or one million. I knew that because I had this conversation all the time.

"The people in sim worlds are not AIs," I explained, gently. "They aren't *people*. They're completely fictional like characters in a novel or a film. They do exactly what the script says. It's just that their script has lots of 'if this' and 'else that' in it, which makes you feel like you're talking to someone who's responding. The game is designed to get you to anthropomorphize the denizens." He appeared confused. "To make you think they're real when they're just emulations - pretend." I paused, trying to think of a good example. "If you don't want bad things to happen to denizens you might as well say you don't want bad things to happen to characters in books." Sandy looked at me as if he might indeed prefer that.

"But they seem real," he protested. "That's why you would never shoot anyone!"

He obviously hadn't upgraded to premium, I thought.

Sandy's father, Stone, broke in. "I think what Lee is saying is that the denizens are not real. They don't have souls like us. Put them in a situation they don't have a script for, and they just stop. Not like a person."

I didn't correct him but that hadn't been what I was saying. Stone was wrong when he said that in a new situation a denizen would just stop. They borrowed from human psychology to handle unfamiliar environments. Nautilus chose a familiar event for our denizen to treat as like the new one they'd encountered.

Say a steam roller was driving towards a denizen version of me. I've never had that happen to me in real life. It would be an unknown situation. Nautilus might tell denizen-me to treat it like a slow-moving car and it would get out of the way rather than hang around to be run over. Sometimes, Nautilus didn't even pick great analogies - they were randomly selected to trigger any action. Ironically, I often thought that was when the denizens seemed most human.

My problem with the denizens was not kidding myself they were real. They were just bits of code with a random number generator in place of free will. They certainly didn't have a magical soul. My problem was wondering how we could know we weren't just characters following a script too. But there wasn't much point worrying about that. What could I do about it?

If denizens were true artificial intelligences, every Lee Sands would probably suspect it was silicon. In almost every world the local version of me created denizens. That might make a true AI doubt its own reality. Fortunately, my denizens didn't live in a state of permanent existential angst because they weren't AIs. They were bots. There's a big difference. They didn't have an internal life to obsess about their internal life. I envied them.

Laura broke into my thoughts. "You said you separate worlds into Utopias and Dystopias. How do you decide what is a good world and what is a bad one?"

I was surprised. Most people didn't ask that, they assumed it was obvious. It wasn't. Over the past ten years, I'd remade the world hundreds of times and in most cases, it wasn't clear whether the update was an improvement on the real world or not.

I told Laura about some of the tools I'd built to help me judge how good a world was. The simplest was what I called my 'Benthamometer'. It used facial emotion recognition. Smiling or laughing denizens were happy. Crying, sneering, or grimacing ones were sad. That was the gist. I used an off-the-shelf sentiment analysis library to do the work. That stuff had been nailed years ago by pre-'36 marketers.

"I can only look at measurable experienced happiness," I told her. "Life satisfaction or remembered happiness isn't something the Panopticon has data on. The denizens can't emulate it."

"How happy are denizens? Or people?" Laura wondered.

I told her it depended when you asked. "Are they eating a doughnut? Or stubbing their toe?"

'How happy is a denizen?' was a more difficult question to answer than it sounds. Over what time period should I sample their apparent emotional states and how frequently? Should I integrate ("Sum up," I said to Sandy when he looked confused) the happiness of a sim world over all of time? Or just for the sim equivalent of today? Or the past week? Or the last year? What about different regions or different cultures? What if half the world was delighted with life and half utterly miserable? How should I weight extremes into the world's happiness score? Was a person crying over the death of their child twice as significant as someone crying from being left by their lover? Or ten times? Or a thousand? What about creatures other than humans?

I told Laura, "So I tried to learn from real examples. I looked at the Hot Summer."

The Hot Summer, as recorded in Control, was great dystopian source material. It was well documented by the Panopticon with plenty of human misery. Easy. 2036 was a dystopia.

However, as soon as things got slightly better, everyone got happy again. The world in '37 was objectively shit, but most people thought it was great compared to running away from a tornado inferno.

When I ran emotional samples on Control in 2037, most people were either dead, in which case they didn't count, or relieved and happy to still be alive. Did that mean '37 was a utopia? Sampling only that year, my happiness algorithms said "yes". At the same time, we hadn't fixed any of our problems yet and most people were living in refugee centres. By no sane measure was '37 a great world. Except for inhabitants comparing it with the previous year.

I described to Laura how I'd wondered if the right algorithm might be inspired by religion. As each denizen died, I could sum up the good and bad emotions they'd experienced throughout their lives and add it to a running score for the world. The problem was that was too long term for the Nautilus worlds. They only stretched back 28 years to when the Panopticon was switched on, any scenes before 2025 were just reconstructions. 28 years didn't give us much full lifespan data.

"Of course," I said, "all those measurements were just for my interest. I finally gave up and we only published the obvious worlds. I decided it was a Dystopia if at least half the populace were running around like rabid zombies and a Utopia if the tech was cool."

Sandy nodded enthusiastically. "Ideally both," he said. He was squarely back in my target demographic.

Ray had been listening quietly during our discussion. "How do you go about it? Decide what changes to make? Given you can do literally anything, where do you even start?"

"I can't actually do *anything*. My brother publicly set some rules." I started to talk about Nemo and his rather restrictive boundaries. They annoyed the hell out of me, but I'd signed up. Without rules the worlds would get out of control. "Nemo's first commandment for world changes," I told Ray, "is 'Thou Shalt Not Break the Laws of Physics'."

That rule thwacked me all the time. I couldn't make stuff appear or create magic new tech. Instead, what I effectively had was a large wad of cash and a time machine. I could go anywhere, look like anyone, and try to be persuasive.

As well as no conjuring, I also wasn't allowed to change the code. Nemo's second commandment was, 'Denizens Are Their Own Masters.' I could bribe them, kill them or threaten them at gunpoint. That was all fine. I just couldn't reprogram them. I couldn't click my fingers and have them do my bidding. That would be cheating. It also wouldn't leave a trail, which would hardly be fair to our detective players trying to track a pivot down.

"So, you aren't a superhero or a God in your virtual worlds," Ray mused. "But you do have loads of dosh and the equivalent of an army of trusted operatives: you can be anywhere at any time and look like anyone. You have full intel and limitless do-overs. Interesting." He produced a lit pipe from somewhere on his person and puffed on it thoughtfully.

Laura and Ray were remarkably astute, I thought. I really needed to get out and talk to real humans more often. And how the hell did he light that pipe?

"Anyway," I continued, shifting about on the hard ground. I looked about and surreptitiously inflated my buttocks. "You asked how I decided what to change."

When I was designing a game, I usually had a final change in mind from the start, but I'd soon realised my desire for a Utopia or a Dystopia made little difference to the result. Bad worlds often came from well-intentioned changes. In fact, more often. Motive didn't much matter. Take anti-aging. In '45 I had an amazing idea how I'd deliver everlasting life to everyone. I intended that world to be my first Utopia. It went terribly wrong. Every way I did it, the world went to hell. Expensive or cheap, slow or fast rollout. It was disastrous. I tried to make that world work for years. I finally gave up and shipped it is a Dystopia.

"Eventually, I accepted the only way to make extended lifespans work is to keep them an expensive secret. Like now," I told Ray. He gave me an odd look.

"Tell me about Control," said Laura. "Have you run your happiness tools on Control?"

"I've run everything there. I use Control all the time for testing stuff," I replied. "Because it shows how people behaved in billions of situations. For the first Dystopia, we needed algorithms for denizen reactions to new events. We got those by watching what they did in similar scenarios in Control." Sandy looked utterly confused, so I explained. "Nautilus generated lots of its code itself. Machine learning."

Sandy was still looking doubtful, so I came up with an example. "In the olden days, we needed to train computers to recognise things from simple photographs." I heard the shire horses whickering behind us. "Take a horse. Imagine we wanted to train a computer to correctly identify a photo of a horse." I pointed at the shires behind us. "Or not a horse." I pointed at Sixpenny and Tenpenny, who were still pulling one another's hair. "The problem is the computer needs a way to infer what a horse looks like because it has no idea."

I was in my stride now. "So, imagine we had a million photos already and some human went through and labelled every one of them as either a horse or not a horse."

"Boring job!" shouted the kids, who were obviously paying more attention than I had given them credit for.

I went on, "Yeah, tedious but it would give the computer something to learn from. We'd give the million labelled photos to our computer and ask it to deduce some rules for deciding if a photo was of a horse or not. Maybe the rules would be it has four legs, pointy ears, a mane and a tail, but who knows. The computer decides. Then we can give it a new photograph. The computer will check the picture against its deduced rules and guess if it's of a horse or not."

"That sounds easy," said Sandy, rather dubiously.

"It is for humans," I replied, "but not for a machine. If you showed it a picture of a bright pink pony it would probably say it wasn't a horse because none of the horses it had photos of were pink. Its rules might say all horses were black or white or brown. To be honest, it's not usually even as simple as that because computers come up with strange rules. They notice weird stuff. The best idea is to give the machine a lot of photos of every possible type of horse if you want it to guess well."

Catterwade spoke to Sandy, "Lee trains the computer to guess whether a new situation is effectively the same as a familiar one. If it is, the denizen can copy their usual behaviour." I nodded. Spot on.

Fortunately, at the end of my digression into computer science Laura was still paying attention so I went back to her question. "You were asking if I'd run the happiness tests on Control, which would really be like running them on the real world?"

"Yes, that's what I'm interested in," said Laura. "You've clearly thought about this a great deal and you have a lot of data to look at. What I would like to know is, do you think we live in a utopia now? Here in the real world?"

I was glad she didn't ask me if we lived in a dystopia.

The problem with the world we currently lived in was it was good in parts. Under the Panopticon, life was fine. People were fairly happy as far as my experiential algorithms could tell. Outside the Panopticon, we had no idea. Everyone could be running around like Mad Max 2 for all most of us knew.

That was one of the reasons I'd given up on happiness measurements. The worlds were always a mixture of happy and unhappy people. How could I decide if it was happy enough? I could take a statistical average. If 99% of people were ecstatically happy and 1% horrifyingly miserable that was a good world.  But was it?  Could you have a statistical utopia that was also a dystopia for some folk?   Should we apply statistics to individuals that way and discount suffering if it only affected a pesky minority?  I just didn't know.

Laura listened to me and then started to tell a story.  "In the 19th Century, a London magazine ran a famous cartoon of a nervous curate having lunch with his bishop.  When it was pointed out that his egg was bad, the curate replied, 'Parts of it are excellent'."  Laura picked up a sock from her mending pile and began to darn it.   "The interesting thing about that is its meaning changed completely over time.  In 1895, it was a joke about excessive politeness.  A rotten egg is obviously entirely bad.  If one part isn't good, the whole thing is undeniably horrid – unless you are too deferential to comment, in which case you have to eat it.   Now though, when people talk about a Curate's Egg, they genuinely mean something that has both good and bad parts.  They view the egg as a utilitarian sum not a binary question.  You are wondering about a real, or imagined, utopia in the same way.  Is it like a real egg? Any rot and the whole thing is bad.   Or is it like the modern Curate's Egg? It can be bad in some parts but good in others."

"That's exactly what I mean!" I yelled. "Are these utilitarian happiness measures a useful tool or a misleading lullaby? Eventually I just threw the whole thing in. I couldn't decide."

We all sat in silence for a second pondering the question.

"I bet they're all happy on Mars," said Sandy. "I would be."

"Actually, it's hard to tell," I responded. "The Mars teams look like they're concentrating so hard all the time their heads might explode. The Earth expression algorithms just don't work there. I think the life is too different. That's another reason not to trust analytics too far. I suspect the people on Mars must be really satisfied with what they're doing. It's difficult, risky, and amazing."

We all sat for another moment contemplating, I suspected, how glad we were that people were colonizing Mars, and that those people weren't us. Except Sandy of course.

"I wish we were on Mars," he said, wistfully.

"Let me take you back to my very first question," said Laura. "What brings you to this place, riding so fast on your shiny bicycle?"  So, I told them all about me, Nemo, and Utopia Five.

Eventually, the moon had risen.  Sandy and the children had gone to their sleeping bags long ago and I wanted to be up at dawn to reach Nemo's place for breakfast.  I thanked Laura, Ray, and their entourage for a fascinating evening.  I hoped we'd meet again someday.

I moved some distance away from the others to sleep in case my would-be nemesis caught up with me in the night.  I pulled up my hood and turned the sensors to maximum range.  That ate battery though.  I tweaked the prox detector code to lower the sampling frequency and cut the drain.

I'd had the suit plugged into my ride all the way here and I'd do the same tomorrow.  I'd streamlined most of the code I was operating on-suit and could run it off the bike indefinitely.  I could practically run it off walking.  Nevertheless, saved power was my safety margin.  You never knew when you'd need it, so I reckoned there wasn't any point wasting it.

Emotionally, I thought, my suit was probably more like my home than my late flat. I'd spent a hell of a lot of time and money upgrading it. It deliberately didn't look that way, there was no point being flashy.

My apartment was merely a convenient Net and power connection. All I needed to access Nautilus, Deus, and everything else on the cloud was built into the suit, along with a serious quantity of solid-state storage. It was my ultimate backup device. I loved it.

Before I closed my eyes, I gave my alert systems twenty minutes to learn the baseline environment: the people, horses, and dogs that were still moving around and the bats that seemed to be going, well, batty round here. I also synced up with the high-level drones and checked online: 50K people were still watching me. I enabled direct alerting for those with a high responsible-citizen quotient. I might as well take advantage of their observation. Then I asked Deus to log everyone still watching if the number fell lower than 10K. My assassin probably wouldn't expose themselves that way, but you never knew. The ground was as dry and hard as the concrete on the road. I added some more adroit padding to the suit and, finally, I slept like a baby - those well-known great sleepers.

# CORNER

## *Analog 2053*

The next morning, I was up and gone as the sun rose and before Laura and her gang had begun to stir.  I wanted to make it to Nemo as early as possible.  At dawn, this far from London the human zones of the road were pleasingly empty.  All I had to dodge were the potholes, which never sleep.  I decided to put my prox sensors on long range and go faster than the 20 mile an hour limit.  The Panopticon would charge me for that, but I wouldn't get any demerits as long as I stayed within safety parameters.

I flipped up my visor, let the wind blow in my face, and thought about my games and the previous night's conversation.  When I created a Utopia, I had to mean it.  I had to work hard to make the world happen and keep it on course.  As I'd told Ray, I couldn't just click my fingers, create a pivot and change the world how I wanted.  Partly that was Nemo and his rules.  As much, it was because there would be no paper trail. No set of clues for players to follow, just a Deus Ex Machina reveal with me as the god outside the virtual machine. I always hated that kind of ending. Nemo and I both agreed it wasn't fair on players. They should get a reasonable "how" as well as a "what" and I thought they should be able to work it out for themselves.

I was, however, still misleading players about how easy it was to create a stable Utopia with a couple of changes. Maybe I'd fooled Nemo too. I could never just kick off the pivot and leave things to play out. If I did, the world ended up a chaotic mess. I had to make small, follow on changes constantly. Utopias needed a lot of maintenance. The tiny tweaks wouldn't be noticeable to the players. I wouldn't expect them to spot them or have the faintest idea they'd happened – but they had.

The Panopticon suddenly broke into my thoughts and suggested I slow down a little as the road started to fill up. The morning was bright with a sharp chill in the air. It was only an hour past dawn, and it was still winter. Most of the people I was passing were wearing coats with their sunglasses.

I pondered the all-seeing-eye's adjustment of my speed. I didn't have to comply, but it helped my social scores if I did, and I knew the recommendation would be based on data I couldn't be bothered analysing myself. I did the same in Utopias all the time. To keep things on track, I planted ideas and made suggestions. There were actions I encouraged or discouraged.

Although Nemo had banned me from controlling denizens, I could still influence what they happened to observe or read as well as nudge them in person. It's amazing how far deeds can be altered by what humans, even emulated ones, see or hear. It doesn't need to break any rules. You don't have to lie to change behaviour. I found truth could be even more effective. I wondered if that was what had gone wrong with Utopia Five. Maybe Nemo hadn't massaged things enough?

My suit flagged up a particularly large pothole ahead. I paid more attention and swerved around it.

The Utopias always needed more management than the Dystopias. A nice society tended to be more organized. That didn't happen by itself. Any big change caused disruption you had to control until you arrived at your new order. Sometimes the disruption in a sim wasn't recoverable.

I moved into the middle lane to pass a herd of cows. Unless they had blinkers on, animals preferred to keep to the inside, well clear of the automated stream that never slowed. I didn't blame them.

I sighed, sadly my best Dystopias usually started from a utopian vision. Occasionally, I had even been able to make a nice idea stick. Eco-worlds were relatively easy for me to deliver. The losers were a small group, which made them tractable. Rich and powerful entrenched interests can be hard to identify and out-maneuver as an individual inside the system, but that was straightforward for a games master. I also boosted space exploration without too much difficulty. That was about getting a limited group of people to spend their money differently.

Whole-society changes were harder. I probably needed much longer to make them work. The 28 years I had in the Nautilus worlds wasn't enough for a big transition that was still gradual enough to not disrupt everything. I wondered if maybe we should try a new series of worlds that went further into the future.

By the time the traffic started to get heavier, I'd turned off the main road. Cycling along quiet country roads in the sunshine was so pleasant it nearly made me forget a killer was on my tail, my company's product was offline, and the longer they both continued the more likely I was to end up dead, bankrupt or both. Of course, 'both' wasn't any worse as I'd no beneficiaries except Nemo and if this did bankrupt me it would be entirely his own fault.

Thinking about my mysterious attempted murderer reminded me. I asked Deus if monitoring the overnight watchers had thrown up anything interesting. I was looking for people who were persistently keeping an eye on me and had been in the vicinity of my London flat within the past few days. They were all potentials as my shadowy nemesis. Deus informed me there were 948 possibilities. I asked it to compile a list of names and photos. I could look through it when I got to Nemo's place and see if I recognized anyone.

As I got closer to the sea the gulls got louder and I could smell the seaweed of the East Anglian coast. The flat, muddy landscape and open skies were not to everyone's taste. I liked it. I could see why Nemo had built his place and come here a year ago.

I would've been happy to go with him when he moved out of our flat. He had never asked. At the time, that hurt. I guess he must have had his reasons. Now he lived in a huge, Bond-villain style mansion in the back end of nowhere. I was surprised he wasn't lonely, but Nemo wasn't much of a people person. I wondered what he was working on now Utopia Five was done.

Finally, around 9:30 in the morning I drew up at the entrance of 'Dangerous Corner', Nemo's giant, semi-subterranean getaway. The solid iron gates seemed taller than I recalled, and he'd really souped up the security. I didn't remember the razor wire fence from last time. There also seemed to be more drones. I guessed now he'd been in the house nearly 12 months I should stop thinking of it as his holiday home. I buzzed the housebot. "It's me, Lee." The gates swung slowly open.

I searched the whole complex. Everywhere. It took hours. I even checked the wardrobes and under the beds. I knew he'd dumped a lot of his Nautilus money into this place, but it was now considerably bigger than I'd imagined. I could see he'd had work done since I was last there maybe six months earlier. It was airtight with bullet-proof quadruple-glazing by the looks of it. Most of the place seemed to be underground.

I went over the lounge first. He appeared to have bought himself several huge sofas, a retractable movie screen, and a deep pile carpet he must have had to wade through. Nemo is not a tall guy. I stared at the soft furnishings. It was so *comfortable* looking. It was almost as if he didn't wear his suit here, but that would be crazy - why would he go off-line like that?

Whatever his inexplicable at-home behaviour, Nemo was clearly not in the house. Damn! I could hardly believe it. I was under the impression he hardly left the place. Where the hell had he gone, just when I needed to get my hands on him?

At least he'd left the electricity and his secure netconn on. I'd really missed a safe connection. Outside Nemo's compound and my own now-smithereen-shaped flat I was uncomfortable about logging onto anything. All the public satellites were notoriously unsecure. I might as well wear my credentials on a sandwich board.

I paused at the edge of a mustard-coloured shag pile rug. Putting my décor inspired horror aside for a moment, I considered. There may be no sign of Nemo there right then, but he couldn't take his data centre with him.

One of Nemo's reasons for moving out here to the middle of nowhere was he'd wanted to build his own private, state-of-the-art, hardware systems. Why? That was anyone's guess. I just hoped what had seemed like a bizarre idea of his a year ago might be about to save my life.

My backup test systems were quite literally fried. His wouldn't be and they were constantly synced with the live servers. I should be able to bring Nautilus back online and operate it from here until I located my little brother and got back onto the Omniscience cloud. I could also access Control and Utopia Five and finally track down the two shadowy figures in my weekend so far: the mysterious watcher in Utopia Five and the person who blew up my house. By lunchtime, I reckoned I could have everything worked out and life nicely back to normal. Maybe I could even try out the home movie system in the afternoon.

Feeling like my problems were nearly over, I took a gold, mirrored lift down into Nemo's nuclear attack proof basement.  It might not be to my taste, but he'd really had everything finished to a high standard.  I was impressed.  Not everyone would take that much care over their bunker.  It only took me another few minutes to get through the airlock, then I was into Nemo's operational facility.  If I hadn't much cared for the reboot of 1975 upstairs, I had total HQ envy over this place.  My tatty living room would have been a complete comparative embarrassment - had it still existed.

I sat down behind the huge, white retro desk of screens that dominated the room.  There were retina scanners and what looked like the kind of two-man-rule control mechanism the old United States used to protect nuke launches. Nice.  Around me in every direction stretched white marble and what looked like endless miles of server racks, but he'd just mirrored the back of the room.  The whole thing was so clean and shiny it was practically lickable.  I did lick it.  It tasted like security theatre.

I got up again, wandered into the racks and plugged my suit directly into a server at random.  If Nemo wanted me to be able to access his machines this would work.  If he didn't then nothing would get me in.  I connected and accessed the orchestration systems, drives and networks.  It was all gone.  He had clearly wiped everything, and he hadn't been subtle about it. From what I could tell, he'd cleaned the whole place out the day before. Just before he'd presumably locked me out of the systems. But why?

I spent the next four hours checking and re-checking every piece of equipment in the entire place. My little brother was nothing if not thorough. It was empty. Damn!

I slumped on one of the giant orange velour sofas in the living room. The only good news was he'd left a lot of snacks in the fridge. Everything else was a disaster. What the hell should I do now? I decided I really had no choice but to talk to God again and this time it would have to be a premium call. I hated those.

# MELTDOWN

## *Analog 2043*

'Global Meltdown' changed everything for Nemo and me. The world discussed it endlessly. I was thoroughly sick of hearing how great President Gates was. I'd only shot the guy in the first place because I couldn't stand him. If it wasn't for Meltdown, he'd probably never have won his second and third terms. There was a lesson there. Nemo and I were suddenly rich though, so I couldn't complain.

Everyone decided they had to try the game and the players were surprisingly good about not revealing the pivot. Every kid who played suddenly wanted to be a detective when they grew up and then realized there was nothing to detect in the real world because the Panopticon did all that and clamoured for Dystopia Two instead. I don't know why it struck the chord it did. It created a new genre overnight: time-travel detection. Wannabe rivals charged towards our niche from every direction at full speed. "Imitation is the sincerest form of flattery," said no IP lawyer ever. Of course, no one else had the Nautilus platform. A few bad copies are really no bad thing at all.

On Nemo's 16th birthday, we graduated from Omniscience Industries' 'Data for Schoolkids' programme and wrote them a mind-boggling virtual cheque for continued access to the OmniscientView. I was not sure that was exactly what they'd had in mind from the initiative. I reckoned it worked out OK for them anyway. At the very least, we all got a lot of publicity.

We churned out four more Dystopias that year and then the same the next. I mean that as dismissively as it sounds. Creating a Dystopia didn't take much effort and they always sold well. I mostly left that to Nemo. He was getting damn good at simultaneously engineering the breakdown of society and the development of whole new areas of weaponry. His autonomous killer underwear was a masterstroke. No one saw that coming, although in retrospect it was obvious that self-cleaning briefs were a dual-use technology.

After we released 'Dystopia Five: Commando Time', WorldGov immediately moved to legislate on nano-laundry tech. Believe me, we did everyone a big favour.

I mostly worked on trying to create Utopias. To be honest, that had been my original aim with Global Meltdown. The road to hell really is paved with good intentions. For every Utopia I managed to stabilize I got four or five Dystopias. We usually published those. It would have been a shame to waste them. They sold very well.

We weren't the only company upping their game. The OmniscientView data feed was getting better. The coverage was improving, and it achieved effective real time. The Panopticon ended up routing the OmniscientView back into Drone Control. That was great for the emergency services. If you collapsed from a heart attack a passing drone could spot it and shock you back to life before you hit the pavement. They electrocuted several people tripping over their shopping before they dialed back those response time targets.

In 2050, the biggest product release was DeusX. Kirby Cross chose that for his new version number rather than Deus10 for some reason. Until '50, God had always been a text message or a voice in your ear that sounded suspiciously like Kirby. DeusX was a fully customizable avatar with augmented reality support. You could talk to God in person in your own living room. Of course, that was a premium feature.

By then, I was starting to get better at Utopias. I never managed to create one where we averted the Hot Summer, it was only ten years between the Panopticon being turned on and the disaster, but I did speed up the re-greening. A decade might not give me enough time to dodge the apocalypse, but I could still drive agri-tech in the right direction to be ready for the rebuild. I could also point the sim's WorldGov in '37 at those fortuitously-ready technologies.

With a bit of judicious pushing and a lot of do-overs, I managed to accelerate the reconstruction efforts by about twenty years. I believe there's a small department at WorldGov devoted to poring over Utopia Four.

I'd found it worked to identify something already happening that I wanted to boost then subtly promote it. Make it happen bigger and faster. That was easier than changing what society wanted in a fundamental way.

We kept at the Nautilus games, releasing a Dystopia every few months and a Utopia every few years until Nemo announced he'd been working on his own Utopia. Utopia Five. He wouldn't tell me his title.

# GOD

## *Analog 2053*

Half-buried in a tangerine-coloured settee, I sat forlornly eating an Omnibar. Nemo had about 30 boxes of the things in the kitchen. Omniscience Industries had recently branched out into confectionery, and we were trying to retrofit more chocolate bars into history. These weren't bad, I thought.

I'd completely run out of ideas. I was used to talking everything over with Nemo and not having him there made me feel sick. Unless that was the chocolate.

I finally reckoned I had no choice. I would have to join the rest of the human race and appeal to my deity for guidance. And this time I'd upgrade.

Since 2050, DeusX had reflected the wisdom and general beliefs of those 70% of the human race who regularly talked to the God-As-A-Service. It wasn't crazy for me to ask for a detailed religious opinion now that I was on a secure line. Especially as Nautilus had coughed up for full enterprise access for both employees. I just didn't happen to usually enjoy the experience.

Everyone who talked to DeusX got the God the engine judged they needed, based on several decades of chat history. They were cagey about how many options they offered. I guessed a few hundred. You didn't get a choice.

I logged in and performed the usual upgrade ritual with my visor down and augmented reality mode enabled. A stout, vigorous woman in her seventies materialized in Nemo's kitchen in front of me.

"Lee, it has been a considerable time since I last saw you. When did you last congress?" my online god demanded, rather sharply.

I must somehow want God to sound like a bossy elderly lady because that's what I got. Margaret Rutherford circa 1964. She was appallingly patronizing, usually right, and never posthumously trademarked.

"Sorry.  It's been 3 months," I apologized.

"We have a great deal of new legislation to go over at the world, regional, and local level.  I hope you have plenty of time!"

Most of us did our democratic duty and regularly talked through governance issues with the digital deity.  Getting out of this was going to cost me a whopping fine and a social demerit.  Never mind, it was my own fault for failing to keep up with my civic responsibilities.  I opted to pay my penance and skip over the legislation review.  I felt a pang of guilt and mentally resolved to spend more time on civics when the current crisis was over.  That was important stuff too.

"So," said my DeusX avatar.  "What do you want to talk to me about?"

I quickly went over the events of the past 18 hours.

"Only Nemo could have locked me out of our systems!  But why would he do that!" I wailed, pathetically.

"Perhaps he left you a note," said God.

"But I'm locked out of the servers!" I wailed, again.

"A real note!  Have you even checked?" God barked.

I found it on the huge white granite kitchen counter, after momentarily wondering why on earth Nemo had such a thing since, as far as I'd observed, he only ate directly from tins.  The note was in his barely legible handwriting.

It read, "Sorry!!"

I spent the next 20 minutes unwrapping every Omnibar in his pristine kitchen and smashing them onto his perfect culinary work surfaces with a rolling pin (why did he even have a rolling pin?)

As I crushed the products of our prime sponsor, whose lawyers would, at that very moment, be drawing up contractual infringement suits against us for our failure to provide an online service, I pondered one of Nemo's key characteristics.  He always kept his work areas spotlessly neat.

Once Nemo had finished working on something, he always put it tidily away back in its proper location. I did not do that. He constantly nagged me about it.

In contrast, the place where I tinkered with new ideas was full of years' worth of detritus. I always vaguely meant to clean it up, but I just ended up buying more storage space. It was easier.

I looked down at my suit. Fortunately, I'd brought my workshop with me. I knew what I was going to do next.

"Did that improve the situation at all?" asked Deus.

"Very much so," I said.

I'd noticed a glitch in Control a few days previously and set up a local test copy to see if I could flush it out. The whole point of Control was to reflect the Panopticon. If it didn't match reality, then there was a problem somewhere. I hadn't had to debug Control in years. Recently I'd noticed a few small discrepancies I wanted to look into.

I'd downloaded a test instance of the Control sim onto my suit drive earlier that week. I'd wanted to sit in the park while I was debugging it, then never got round to doing the work and forgotten all about the copy. Someone had locked me out of the live worlds and all the test ones were deleted or blown up. My offline version, however, was still there.

My Control copy had been last synced too long ago to teach me much about the explosion. It could, however, still tell me about something else.

"Deus, when did Nemo write this note?"

"11:45 pm, 2 days ago."

"Thank you very much."

*ControlTest 2053, 2 Days Ago*

I watched the denizen version of Nemo standing in his kitchen writing a note. I was about to magically appear in front of him.

In real life this would be somewhat of a surprise. Personally, I find people seldom mysteriously materialise before me. On the Nautilus platform, however, it was one of our few suspensions of Nemo's laws. You can enter a world anywhere you like and stay invisible there as long as you please and then appear without terrifying the local populace. All denizens have a "don't-freak-out!" behavioural override for materializations. We didn't have that in Dystopia 1 and users complained they had to spend half their game time looking for trees to appear behind.

"What the frack does 'Sorry!' mean!?" I yelled at this faint copy of the target of my wrath.

"Hi Lee, that's a very interesting question. From your sudden appearance I assume I'm a denizen. Which world?" asked Nemo.

"Control." Which was nearly true. I never worried too much about lying to denizens and I didn't have time for a lengthy explanation.

I know people find it hard to believe denizens are not AIs. It's human nature to anthropomorphize. Nemo and I wrote the code. We know they're chatbots – just thoroughly trained ones.

We're still miles off general AI and I don't believe we have the power required for it now, at least outside the MegaCorps. Nonetheless, contrary to his own rules, Nemo definitely hacked about with his game selves. They were always disturbingly sophisticated. He was more than capable, and it would be in character to screw with me. I say me because I was pretty much the only human his personal denizens talked to.

Nemo gazed down at the piece of paper on the counter in front of him. "Frankly," he said, "I have no idea why I just wrote this note. We only have that to go on," he waved a hand at the kitchen Panopticon camera and mic. "And unlike some people, *I*," he said while pointing theatrically at his own chest. "Don't go in for a lot of expository soliloquies so I've no idea why I did what I just did."

That was a dig at me. Virtual Nemo did have a point. Most of us had got into the habit of explaining our thought processes out loud to the all-seeing-eye. The Panopticon couldn't see what we were thinking so we told it. We were like Richard Nixon on steroids. It felt like a duty to record everything we said, did, or merely pondered for posterity. We were hooked on exposition. Perhaps how things turned out for Nixon should have taught us something about the dangers of constantly taping yourself. I suspect it just demonstrated that humans always believe their actions to be justified. My brother, I had noticed, never explained his motives. He liked to be enigmatic. Or just annoying.

"You know," I said, "When you told me you had an idea for a Utopia I was surprised. In ten years, you'd never shown any interest in the non-combat sims."

"Well, that wasn't unreasonable," he replied. "The Dystopias are fun, easy, and make us a load of money." He jumped up and sat on the counter with his legs dangling down. "You know, I always suspected meddling in events only made things worse in the long run. Omission beats commission."

I obviously disagreed. I liked to interfere. "Then why create a Utopia? And why are you making things so difficult right now?" I asked.

"I'm afraid that's something he never shared with me. You'll have to find the real Nemo and ask him. My guess is he wanted to test out one of his theories. You know him better than I do. After all, I'm just a chatbot."

I sighed.

"I do know one thing," he said, looking like he was taking pity on me. "You know how lucky we were with Dystopia One?" I nodded and he continued, "We've learned a lot since then. Some points in history are much easier to pivot – moments when anything could happen."

I agreed. It was a combination of society, or enough of it, wanting changes and lots of people with influence coming together in one place. A confluence of need, money, and power.

"At those times, a word or action can change everything," he said.

The real Nemo had called these points "dangerous corners" after some old play. Mostly they were treacherous. It was very hard to create a Utopia out of a dangerous corner, but imagine what it would look like if you could? The odd thing was those moments often looked quite alike.

The fake Nemo continued, "I know he has been thinking a lot about those points in time. I think he'd found something." I looked expectant, "I don't know what it was," he said. "Sorry."

I exhaled. That was an anti-climax. "If you don't know what Nemo's up to either, I can't log into the live servers remotely, and there's nothing left to access here then I guess I've no choice about what to do next."

"You're off to see the Heavenly Host," said my pseudo-sibling.

"Yes."

# DYSTOPIA

*Analog 2052*

Nemo was a master of the malign. His ability to bring about truly disturbing weaponry was unparalleled. The last few Dystopias introduced his new bio/nano fusion infections, and the games were so stomach-turning they came with health warnings. Our players physically threw up. It was fantastic. They loved them.

'Dystopia 37: Who's Laughing Now?' was one of my all-time favourites. Stealth-infected, evil body parts. It was a good job most users hadn't installed the ear wiggling avatar extension. I fainted. I guess Nemo had never really forgiven me for that workaround.

When he said he was working on a Utopia, I was torn about whether to give him some of my tools.

In ten years, I'd only managed four Utopias and it wasn't like I hadn't tried. They were just bloody hard to create. I think we underestimate how much small but widespread pressure real humans exert towards order. The algorithms don't pick it up just from tracking the behaviour they observe. The Panopticon would need to know what we were thinking and why we did what we did. Mostly we didn't even know that ourselves and it wasn't obvious from our actions.

To program denizens who could steer the world towards order, I reckoned Nautilus would need to know what their human counterparts were anticipating three, four or five steps ahead. For some people, I suspected, each decision was part of a multi-year plan inside their heads that the Panopticon remained completely unaware of. If that wasn't the case, the real world would be chaos.

Over the years I'd made a few tools to help me build Utopias. The problem was, Nemo might have considered them cheating. I didn't think they were against the rules, but he was such a stickler. If I'd told him he might have banned them, so it seemed safer to let him go it alone.

As I informed Laura and Ray, we say the world in our games is changed in a single pivotal moment. It isn't really. There's always one iconic big change like shooting a President or inventing a marvelous new bit of tech. That's what the users uncover when they play detective and investigate. In fact, to make a world coherent with a storyline and an overarching vision we need to keep guiding it. An initial push is not enough. Perhaps in the real world with real humans it would be. I don't know. I do know that denizens don't anticipate three steps ahead or have a mental five-year plan. They don't keep things stable.

Denizens are not humans or AIs. I'm not saying they're random gas particles - they make sensible, plausible moves dictated by the algorithms. It's just not enough. If I want to produce an orderly world, I have to keep herding it back on track. The denizens don't pick up any of that slack and they do anarchic stuff most real humans would never contemplate. You have to watch them constantly. Utopias need a lot of maintenance.

# HOST

## *Analog 2053*

*The Heavenly Host*, I thought.

I wouldn't put it past virtual Nemo to report what I was about to do to my real brother. I quickly cut off outbound Net access from the Control sim on my suit. It might already have been too late. I'd always suspected the Nemos were snitches.

I flicked up my visor and returned to my brother's kitchen in the real world. I was mildly surprised his denizen knew where the physical

Nautilus systems were. We hardly ever talked about them. I was regularly reminded of their existence by the huge invoices - if the divine word didn't come cheap, neither did the host.

Despite Nemo's swanky white HQ in his basement and my now-destroyed systems in London, we didn't run the huge machines that powered Nautilus Games ourselves. Like everyone else, we let Omniscience Industries do it for us. We called them the Heavenly Host.

Using the OmniscientView video feeds meant a hell of a lot of data to move between their servers and ours. Way too much to pass over the public lines. For Control to stay real time, we needed our machines sitting in the same building as Omniscience's with a bloody thick cable between. We weren't the only ones who had arrived at this revelation. All the MegaCorps had embraced the divine host. Kirby displayed his normal wisdom and exacted a tithe. It cost ten percent of your revenues to use Omniscience's servers with their superfast access to the Panopticon data. We paid up and were thankful.

My next step to get the Nautilus systems back online was inevitable. As virtual Nemo had guessed, if I couldn't get to our machines over the

Net, I would have to visit the Heavenly Host myself. The result of monthly bills the size of ours was there were a lot of people at Omniscience very happy to help me remain a customer. The problem was remote contact with them clearly wasn't going to cut it. I doubted even I could engineer an administrative coup on our hardware over the phone. They had my physical metrics on file. I was just going to have to go and press some flesh.

I pulled up a map of Britain on my visor. Everyone knew where the Heavenly Host was. Five years ago, Kirby Cross had consolidated Omniscience Industries' worldwide operations at one location. He bought a large island off the west coast of Britain and moved his staff and machines there. Few people entered his HQ stronghold if they didn't work for Cross and his employees lived there behind the firewalls. He renamed the place Angelsea, demonstrating money doesn't buy taste.

I would have to get in and persuade the Oompa Loompas to take my fingerprints.

It should take me four days to get to Angelsea if I picked up a few speeding fines. This trip was severely denting my social responsibility scores.

I decided not to take the bus. With a murderous bomber in pursuit, I suspected I was a menace to public transport. Anyway, I might need the bike and it was a good way to charge the suit.

I realized I'd need some provisions for the trip and the Omnibars were off the table or, in fact, mashed onto the table. I opened some of Nemo's cupboards. He didn't disappoint me. I grabbed handfuls of freeze-dried food rations and a nanofilter water flask. You could sit out a nuclear war in this place, I thought, plus sea views. I had to hand it to Nemo, it really was a great holiday home.

I'd given up chasing my brother around the country, but I queried his current location with Deus anyway. It was still registering as this house. That meant he must have left via the secret passageway and donned a disguise before he emerged. I nodded to myself. Old school. The entrance was hidden in one of the basement toilets. I'd checked the passage already. His dead body wasn't lying in it with the life choked out or anything. That would be my job when I finally caught up with him.

I had one task remaining before I left. I scanned the list of my persistent watchers from last night, which Deus had cross-referenced with people who'd been in North London in the past few days. I speed-read through every name, photo, and bio, trying to spot something I recognized. A face caught my eye. Wigborough Wick, 48, a maths teacher. Like everyone else on the list, he sounded innocuous.

I left Nemo's Dangerous Corner six hours after I'd arrived. I thought about sleeping there in a real bed but had five hours of daylight left. I wanted to use them, and I didn't want to stay in one place long enough for my nemesis to catch up.

I'd no idea what resources they had. The bomb the previous day had been improvised, which didn't suggest a large, well-funded organization. I would have suspected a stalker, except for the systems lockout and, of course, the police wouldn't know about that. If I'd died the crank idea would have seemed highly plausible. Had that been the intention? In which case, it could be a large organisation pretending to be a lone nutcase. This was doing my head in. It all sounded like one of Nemo's Dystopia plots.

I set off cycling roughly west at high speed along the country lanes. The route across the country was slow. There weren't many major roads from my brother's place to Wales, so public transport would have been tricky even if I'd been happy to use it. I wasn't. The risks were too high with an obvious, well-defined route. I didn't want to end up in a shootout on a double decker bus full of grannies.

As I rode, my prox detectors - combined with a direct link to the high-level drones - kept me aware of what was coming ahead. I added some random diversions into my route. One of the benefits of staying off the motorways was my exact path would be hard to predict. Any planned attack on me would require changes to the normal behavioural patterns on multiple roads and be easier for my scanners to spot.

The weather was warm and only slightly windy. No more than 40 knot gusts. As good as I could hope for. The suit's heat exchanger cooled me down and heated up the phase change materials in the core. They'd keep me warm overnight as the temperature and my activity levels dropped. In summary, perfect conditions.

I could hear the sounds of wildlife around me. The animal population had restored itself since '36, insects and birds benefiting from some change. Environmentalists speculated it was the now-lightless nights. There were so many differences since the Hot Summer it was hard to know. I cycled fast through a cloud of dragonflies. For a moment, I thought it was an attacking swarm of microdrones. It wasn't. I could see the invertebrates splattered on my visor. I wiped them off with the back of my glove and felt slightly guilty. Death by speeding bike helmet wasn't usually part of the natural cycle of life.

Nearly four hours later, I was thinking about breaking for a food ration when one of my high-trust followers sent me an alert. There was something interesting about a mile ahead, off my projected track on a wider road. I connected into the local drone feeds and looked. It was a motley camp of people, tents, dogs, and wrestling children that I recognised.  I wondered what Laura, Ray and their travelling band were doing there and where they'd got the couple of large trucks from.  Those looked official.

As night fell, I was sitting around a stove with my companions from the previous night.  Oddly, they didn't look surprised to see me.  A few hours earlier the line walkers had got an alert about a problem in Northwest Wales.  The Panopticon would provide transport to any qualified personnel happy to drop everything and hightail it there.

"Laura volunteered!" Sandy declared.

The lorries had picked them up and this was as far as they'd got.  Catterwade and Stone were bringing the horses and wagons behind.  They might even catch up.

By strange coincidence, we were all travelling to the same place.  North Wales.  Home of the most important network hub on the planet: Omniscience's island HQ.

"You can wiggle your ears!" shouted one of the kids.  It was just my sixth-sense tingling.

# ERGODICITY

*Analog 2053*

An hour later, I'd brought out the whisky from my bike. I needed it. Ray had produced some glasses.

"So," he said, "can you predict the future with Control? Could you run a gambling empire?" He had obviously been thinking about our last conversation. I didn't mind being interrogated. I liked to discuss the games and I'd missed having Nemo to talk to.

I told Ray for individuals in an isolated environment we could predict events for a short period. Sub second. Longer than that, it was like playing a single shot of billiards. "It sounds simple," I said, "but even in perfect conditions there are too many random elements. You can't predict where your ball will end up after only a couple of bounces. It's so sensitive to tiny changes, you'll never play exactly the same shot twice, even from identical starting points."

"Like ergodicity," said Sandy. "'The state of an ergodic process after a long time is nearly independent of its initial state.' You can't predict it. We did it at school."

I might have to hire Sandy, I thought.

"Is what you're saying that anything that can happen will happen?  Eventually, anyway," mused Laura, digging a T shirt out of her mending pile. "Doesn't that mean you don't actually have to alter much in the past of your sims? The tiniest change could roll up to something huge?"

"The famous butterfly flapping its wings and causing a tornado?" I replied.  "You're right.  It's just as unpredictable as that.  Worse, because we have to inject randomness into every choice to make the behavioural algorithms work.  That means simulated interactions between denizens have a lot more possible outcomes than balls bouncing off cushions on a pool table."  I took a swig of my whisky.

"None of the denizen models work without random number generation," I continued.  "Even if initial conditions were identical – which is something we can deliver in a sim – the final state wouldn't be the same. In reality, I don't have to make any deliberate change at all in a game world. If I let the behaviour engine take over and run events, the sim immediately starts to diverge from reality."

A quiet voice sounded from the far side of the circle. It was the normally silent Catterwade. "That sounds like thermodynamics. Do your worlds descend into chaos over time? I wonder if that's why you get more Dystopias than Utopias." She paused, thinking. "Have you tried running the projections further forward into the future?"

Laura put down her sewing and chimed in. "The interesting question is, is an emulated system more likely to become chaotic than a human one? We only have one real world and that's relatively orderly by the sound of it, at least compared to your Dystopias?" I nodded. "That seems statistically fortuitous. Perhaps that is Stone's proof that humans have souls? Or at least we guide the world towards some degree of order. Are we agents of order? It doesn't always feel that way!"

She laughed, but there was something in her words and I mused aloud. Why was reality so neat compared to most of our game worlds?  At least, the real world seemed well-organised in the Panopticon regions.  Emergent behaviour of some sort?  An invisible hand?  If we were merely genetically programmed to be orderly in our behaviour, like ants, surely the Nautilus algorithms would pick that up and denizens would be as good agents of order as humans?

"Have you modelled any ants?" Catterwade asked.  I shook my head.  "If you did simulate them," she continued, "would their worlds stay on track or descend into insect chaos? That would be interesting to know."  She looked at me challengingly.  "If they did fall apart, I suspect there might be something wrong with your machine learning because ants seem to manage fine.  If there were a guiding force in human or ant behaviour, shouldn't that get included in what your algorithms learned from the Panopticon, so you'd emulate it in the sims?"

These people were really putting me through my paces.  "Perhaps.  It would depend how the force worked.  Whether it was consistent and had been repeated over and over in the past - like genetic programming - or something sporadic and random. Not obvious from the context," I replied.  "Humans are probably driven by both.  Ants, maybe, less so."

"So, why do you make your 'pivots' when you don't need to do anything at all for your worlds to change?" asked Ray, leaning forward and taking the subject back to something more practical.

"It wouldn't be much of a game otherwise," I replied. "We need a storyline. There's nothing wrong with social psychology experiments, but they don't pay the big bucks."

# REFUGEES

*Analog 2038*

Like all the urban areas, when Nemo and I arrived in London in 2038 it was bulging at the seams with refugees.  The city leaders suddenly had to feed and house a million frightened people from all over Britain.  Everything was in disarray and the government was overwhelmed.

The London authorities decided they needed complete control over their fate, and they took it.  They nationalized land for the new city state, cleared it where necessary, and built homes and shelters using the huge workforce of displaced citizens they'd just acquired.  As part of the new arrivals, Nemo and I joined in the effort.  That was the easy part.

When we weren't helping to sweep up and wash dishes in the care centre, the two of us logged in for school like we always had.  I remember we all spent a lot of time in '37 writing reports on agricultural theory.    I guess that'd suddenly become more pressing than the history of Tudors and Stuarts.

"For over 300 years," I typed, "human progress has been about upgrading every activity we can think of from slow organic labour to fast mechanised power.  All driven by stored energy. We found most of that in fossil fuels."   Huge machines had produced the stupendous quantity of food and goods humanity needed.  More of them delivered the stuff vast distances to the individuals who consumed it.  It all worked, and it all needed fuel.

Our survival had depended for years on powered machinery and logistics. The Hot Summer hadn't changed that, and we didn't know what to do about it yet.

Unsurprisingly, after the chaos and destruction of '36 most of the terrified populace wanted to ban hydrocarbons immediately.  At school we talked a lot about how it wasn't that straightforward.  I think the kids were supposed to go home and educate their families on the reality of the situation: we already had food shortages, but things could get worse.  The fuels had killed a billion of us but kept the remaining ones alive. We had no clue how to live without them.

Between the Panopticon supernation, the schools, and the city assemblies, we managed to find a way forward. The old fuels were rationed for their most important purposes: replacing themselves and keeping us fed and educated during the transition.

As far as Nemo and I were concerned, the most interesting change was the new non-essentials law. Cooking, heating, and aircon were immediately rationed. In the refugee centres, we were already eating in community kitchens and living in the halls. The new rules didn't make much difference to us, but they did mean lots more people came into our dining rooms for dinner. We started eating at strange times to avoid the crowds. Next, cars were practically banned. People realized if you couldn't get somewhere by bike or on foot you weren't going. We were too young to drive and the centres had plenty of carts and bicycles. We thought the empty roads were amazing - for about a month. They soon filled up with a crazy variety of makeshift vehicles. We thought they were cool too.

By 2038, every spare bed in the city had a lodger or two in it and the new dormitories were full to bursting. Nemo and I liked the full halls at the refugee centres. There were always interesting people to talk to and we were both alive. What was so terrible about squeezing top to tail into a bunk? Nemo was pretty shrimpy anyway, and it wouldn't be forever.

The civil stuff was decided by the new city-wide Panopticon congresses. It was inevitable. The chaos had broken our global supply chains. Only one thing was sure: we were all going to get a lot thinner.

Within a year, most of the cities had expanded their guarantee of food and housing from refugees like us to everyone. That headed off a lot of ill-feeling. You didn't get a wide array of choices in where you stayed or what you ate but you did get something and with the Panopticon back in place to keep its hovering eye on the populace, we discovered it's amazing how much you can achieve when no-one can cheat.

Ironically, our rebuilt cities were wood. We'd learned a lot about fire control during the Summer. We'd had to. We could make even wooden cities safe if we planned them well and monitored them like crazy. The good news was we liked monitoring things. Every drone continued to be part of the fire watch.

It turned out some enterprising individual had always rescued leftovers from the great felling and kept them safe. Those folks probably didn't make as much money from the last remaining timber as they'd hoped, but I'm sure they felt great about their contribution to the public good.

Wood was now our material of choice. We knew the felling would come back to bite us. We needed new trees and we used every spare inch of land for them that could be planted safely. As soon as new wood was grown, we planned to harvest it, build with it, and replant. The re-greening started in 2037. It quickly spread to the oceans where we cultivated huge areas of seaweed and algae for food.

New construction, planting, fire regulation, and clearance kept people busy. On the video feeds we could all see outside the cities, on the seas and in the countryside, the focus on food and logistics. We agreed, the old fuels were best reserved for that.

By 2039 we had enough to feed a considerably slimmer population. Finally, we turned our attention to the progress on Summer control and we weren't happy. Bureaucracies aren't known for their speedy action and it became clear national governments weren't going to be enough. They were too big to coordinate local action and too small to handle the big decisions. By 2040, the Panopticon assemblies had spread to every functioning region left on earth and an overseeing WorldGov was in place. For the first time, Earth was united. At least, what was left of it.

Once the initial struggle was over, we started to think about normal life again. In Britain, if you lived anywhere south of Edinburgh then no aircon got highly uncomfortable at times. It could still feel really cold too. We all missed central heating. I'd never fully appreciated the humble radiator.

Then some bored US dude read Dune. He talked to his local Panopticon assembly and, after a few false starts, the stillsuits started to appear. Nemo was a huge classic science fiction fan. He was desperate to get his hands on one. The suits made perfect sense. The idea came from a 1960's SF novel about people living on an overheated desert planet. Sound familiar? The UK wasn't anything near that bad but great swathes of the world were. I could see why Dune caught people's attention.

Stillsuits were hooded leather bodysuits with a layer of water bladders next to your skin. Making them work in real life required a little more engineering than the original author had envisaged, but collectively we got it working. The suits were more efficient at managing the temperature of a human than warming or cooling a whole building. Just don't ask where the water in the bladders came from. Actually, in the UK we used the tap.

Heating, cooling, and water re-use. All built into leathers. It was local and efficient. We all looked like futuristic biker gang members, but I never thought that was a bad thing. Nemo and I contributed some of the control code and in return we got a couple of early versions.

We were converts as soon as we tried them on.

# A LIFT

*Analog 2053*

The next morning, I loaded my bike into the back of one of the trucks. As we were going the same way, Laura had offered me a ride. It was still going to take three days to reach Angelsea - the lorries were human-driven, and we had equipment to collect on the way. The lift wasn't going to speed up my journey, but I had decided to take it anyway. It would give me time for the research I desperately needed to do.

I settled onto a hard seat against the side of the lorry and strapped in. We wouldn't be moving fast; the vehicles weren't autonomous, so we were limited to the organic road space. Even at our slow speed though, it would be tough to avoid the potholes. I expected it would be a bumpy ride and enabled the Michelin feature on my suit. Since the collapse of the tire market, who would have guessed that would become their entire business? They didn't even have to change the logo.

Feeling slightly more comfortable, I pulled down my visor. I needed to know what my brother had been doing for the past six months. Where in hell had Utopia Five taken him? I still had the Control copy I'd found on my suit the day before. It was now 48 hours out-of-date. That wouldn't matter for what I intended.

# ZOOM

## *ControlTest 2053*

That morning, I watched the last 200 days of my brother's life, in reverse, at one minute per day. After three hours my head was exploding, and I had an excellent idea what he'd been up to. The problem was it was excruciatingly dull. It didn't explain Utopia Five or the lockout. I had to be missing something.

At least I had complete coverage of Nemo. That had surprised me. I'd always suspected my brother resented the Panopticon, yet it appeared he'd had cameras and microphones installed in every room of his new place. It was odd.

It wasn't compulsory to film yourself in private, but your trust score would take a hit if you didn't - you might leave the tap running while you brushed your teeth for Deus' sake. 'What do you have to hide?' ran the advertising campaign for Omnipresent, the biggest-selling household monitoring system. I'd never thought my brother was bothered about social acceptability or ratings though because he used to tear those posters down.

Nemo's house was surprisingly fully recorded but he was sneaky at hiding from the Panopticon when he wanted, so I hadn't expected the whole story to unfold for me on film. That would be too easy. I was relying on him making a mistake. What I didn't see should be as revealing as what I did. There should be days with less footage of him. That was when he'd be up to something. My plan was to focus on those missing times. I guessed there would be scraps of intel at the edges.

I found nothing. He had been on camera constantly for 200 days. Nemo, pottering around his 70's shag pile mansion like Elvis brought back from the dead 6 inches shorter, a hundred kilos lighter and with no musical talent or sideburns. Perhaps not that much like Elvis. Apart from the home furnishings.

There were no missing days. No missing time. Damn! It made no sense!

I randomly picked a day. He was lounging around in a dressing gown in the kitchen, reading on a tablet. I switched focus to his screen. "Zoom and enhance," I said.

I have a confession to make. I hated losing to my brother. One of us would write a game. The other would beat it. That's what we did. The last few, Nemo had been getting too good. He scared me.

That deranged cleaner at Microgenics Corp with a doctorate in nanobacterial engineering and a secret Bruce Campbell fixation? I nearly gave up. How Nemo had even found the guy, never mind transformed him into an evil mastermind. That was genius. After Dystopia 37 came out, Microgenics sent the sanitation engineer to counselling and promoted him to head of research. Astute PR on their part. I hoped he was well monitored.

After that near failure I wanted an ace up my sleeve for his next game, so I paid the Panopticon to double its surveillance resolution on Nemo. Money isn't everything. Winning is.

When I said, "Zoom and enhance." It should work.

## ControlTest 2053

I was finally going to find out what my brother was investigating. Nemo's screen leapt into view. It was the main page of the Panopticon state news broadcaster. Nemo was cheerfully drinking coffee and reading the lead story. It was about an angry-looking cat stuck in a tree.

Nemo watching porn or reading comics I'd believe. Feel good news about cute animals? I didn't think so. I'd learned a lot of disturbing things about him in the past two days. This would be a whole new level. I knew my brother and I'd bet my life this wasn't reality.

I zoomed out. There was a clock on the gold kitchen wall conveniently in view and synced with the Panopticon time stamp. Unenhanced, I could make out enough of the screen on the table to correlate the headlines with the time and date of the recording. I could even see the weather through a huge plate window. I guessed it would match local met conditions if I checked. It was all extremely convincing. Too convincing. It would damned well have to be.

Omniscience deployed their first video fraud alert systems in 2032. Since then, a lot of people have tried to feed bad data to the Panopticon. As far as we knew, they had never pulled it off.

If Nemo had convinced the all-seeing-eye of the Panopticon that a faked-up sim was reality, every criminal mastermind left in the world would want the technology. The existence of this tech would undermine everything we'd built since '36. We relied on trust in the Eye. Why on earth would Nemo create something so dangerous? I hoped he wasn't flirting with the collapse of civilization to hide his browsing history.

I'd no doubt my brother had created a way to fool the Panopticon. The question was why. What was he hiding? Whatever it was, he was doing it irritatingly well. I needed to take a different approach.

I stopped and thought. There must have been a point when Nemo didn't know he was going to build Utopia Five. He might not have been hiding his activities yet, unless he did that all the time. I desperately hoped he saved his world-destroying invisibility trick for important stuff.

Late the previous summer, Nemo had started to talk about a Utopia. Maybe he'd got an idea from something he'd seen around that time? I would begin there.

# TIME TRAVEL

## Control 2045

In the early days of Control, I'd tried a couple of times to convince a denizen version of me that I was them from the future and they had to rob a bank for whole-future-depends-on-it reasons. To see what would happen.

Of course, if the world had been locked nothing did happen. They dismissed the whole thing and went on with their storyline. It was more interesting if I made the intervention a pivot and forced the world to recalculate from that point onwards.

Disappointingly, that pivot never worked on my denizens. All the mes remembered the "I'm you from the future!" pranks from 2026. After the Panopticon data went open a load of apps found people who looked like younger versions of you. It was funny for a while. Everyone wised up quick. A few people went to prison, but the courts were surprisingly sympathetic. They discussed adding "because you thought the world was at stake" as a legal defense but decided gullibility was not a valid excuse for grand theft.

I reckoned I could still have persuaded a version of myself I was from the future if I could have revealed some coming events. Surely that's what sports were for? Nemo kyboshed that. He was such a stickler for the rules. If your pivot injected a spoiler and broke the timeline your new world wouldn't save. I'm not ruling out the possibility of time travel. Personally though, if this ever comes up for me, I'll demand at least some racing tips before I commit any felonies.

# JUDGEMENT

*Analog 2053*

While I was logged into my Control copy, the trucks made steady progress on the back roads. I was still wading through the life of Nemo when Ray tapped me on the shoulder. We were stopping.

Some civic responsibilities outweigh everything else and one of those is a distress call. The village we were passing was broadcasting a request for the aid of a judge. They were outside the jurisdiction of the city states in the area and had to source their own judiciary. Someone must have set up an alert for a likely candidate that flagged Laura when we passed. They sent her a direct plea and now we were obliged to halt. Who knew when another judge would pass by?

"Laura is qualified to dispense justice on behalf of the Panopticon?" I said to Ray. "That's high-level stuff."

"You've no idea," he replied. "We get called to handle disputes all the time. They could sort it out legally with a remote official, but sometimes emotions run high. They need someone in person to calm things down."

Most of our decision-making was by debate, research, and ballot. The idea of a single person deciding the rights or wrongs of a situation seemed bizarre. Why would strangers let Laura choose their fate when a remote lawbot could adjudicate or the whole village could vote?

We turned off our route and detoured to the source of the distress call. At this rate, Stone, Catterwade, and the horses would catch up by dusk. The trucks drew up in the main square. We parked and stepped out into blazing sunshine. Our destination turned out to have the inauspicious name of Furnace. It certainly was hot.

The roads of the village were dry and dusty, and the green wasn't named well. I wondered if I'd be better off inside watching Nemo. I was already most of the way through August 2052 and I'd found nothing. Time was running out. I had to work out what my brother was planning but I decided a break focussed on something outside of my own helmet might help.

I looked around at the village. Maybe Furnace wasn't such a bad name after all. It was alive with tech. Every roof was solar. I could see windmills, and a major battery array off the square. Alongside that was a row of huge agridomes filled with greenery. Half a mile off I spotted the glint of fishing lakes. Deus told me they were fed by a small river and this was a phase 3 independent community, 76.3% self-sufficient.

Down a side street leading away from the so-called green, I noticed a scowling woman of around sixty. She was waving and beckoning us towards a cottage. I had expected someone more official-looking.

The others looked unfazed and formed a semi-regal procession with Laura at the front, followed by Ray and Sandy. I'd a feeling they'd done this before. The three drivers had clearly decided to disappear into the local pub. The rest of us picked up Laura's mood. Even Tenpenny and Sixpenny looked severe. I fell into step behind them.

"Everyone is always frowning when we arrive," whispered Tenpenny, leaning back towards me as we walked.

"How about when you leave?" I asked.

She looked a bit pensive, "Well, it varies."

Sixpenny nodded in agreement and pointed at her running shoes. That didn't fill me with confidence.

We followed our angry-looking summoner up a garden path fringed with wilted spring flowers. Laura strode through the front door of the single-story house and everyone crowded in behind her. I hung back but Sixpenny and Tenpenny grabbed my arms and dragged me inside.

The entrance opened into a sitting room full of outsized furniture, which looked like it had been inherited from several mismatched sources. Through an open door I could see a kitchen and garden beyond. I was crushed against a three-piece suite and Sandy and Ray were balancing precariously around a glass-topped coffee table, trying to give Laura enough room to look official. An old lady in a wheelchair was similarly shoehorned in and looking defiant.

"Right!" declared Laura, "My first pronouncement is that we should move to the garden."

Five minutes later, we had relocated to the small lawn at the back of the cottage. Laura and the frowning woman perched on sun loungers and the elderly lady sat in her wheelchair. The rest of us arranged ourselves behind the judge.

"Why have you called on me, a representative of both law and judgement?" intoned Laura, addressing the younger of the two women. I was impressed. She clearly knew how to put something like this across.

"It's my mother," she replied, "She's gone crazy!"

We all turned to stare at the woman in the wheelchair, whom we assumed was the lunatic described. She looked resolute rather than deranged.

"I would like to hear from the accused party." Laura gestured towards the mother, who sat up straight and cleared her throat.

"My name is Elizabeth Whiteacre.  I am 91 years of age and until five years ago I was the headmistress of the local school."  She paused and looked piercingly at each of us.  "I now live with my daughter and I have submitted a request for the services of an official undertaker.  I have thought about this thoroughly.  My time has passed, and I no longer warrant the energy I require to live.  My daughter is very fond of me and I of her.  This is, however, my decision."

Laura listened carefully to the woman's statement before reaching down and pulling a sophisticated-looking visor from her capacious sewing bag.  She put it on, paused for a moment as if reading, then spoke.

"It is true that a price is paid for every human to live but they also contribute."  Laura looked closely at the old woman, who held the gaze.  "I can see your past work was highly valuable, you are clearly not considering that."  Mrs Whiteacre firmly shook her head.  "Therefore, neither will I," Laura continued.  "Let us judge only the current and future times."

Laura held out her left arm and the fabric of her cloak-like coat fell beneath it to the grass.  On what was clearly a folding screen, a picture of a set of scales appeared. One side of the balance showed the face of the daughter on the other side the mother.

"Your death would sadden your daughter greatly." The scale fell as if weighed down by the grief of the younger woman. "But you feel guilt and shame at your own lack of contribution." The scales fell on the other side, bringing the system into balance. "Elizabeth Whitacre, you are clearly of sound mind. If you would delay your call to an undertaker the Panopticon would welcome your eyes and mind in its work, which is of significant worth." The scales wavered. "But that is a decision for you alone."

Laura turned to us five, standing behind her. "Lee, can you return Sandy and the girls to the lorries and see if you can find us some dinner? Ray and I will be a little longer."

Thus, dismissed from the adult conversation, we traipsed back. Ray and Laura appeared an hour later. Laura pled tiredness and disappeared into the back of the truck, while Ray and I took the children to the pub in search of the drivers and some sandwiches. I decided not to ask what the Whiteacres' decision had been.

"How long would they have to wait for an undertaker to pass by here?  Might it be a long time?" I asked.

"I am an undertaker," Ray replied.

# NEMO

## *Analog 2053*

We set off intending to drive until dark, and I returned to my copy of Control to review Nemo's actions from before he'd had anything to hide. I needed to explain my brother's behaviour quickly, not least because whoever was chasing me would eventually catch up. I buckled myself into a seat and pulled my visor into place. I had a week left to watch of Nemo's August 2052. I fervently hoped it would tell me something.

Apparently, my brother spent a lot of his time reading in the kitchen. I guessed that was the behaviour he would simulate whenever he needed to disappear. Like his subsequent six months, most of the recordings of him in August '52 were this manufactured newspaper browsing. Deus knows what he was really up to.

On the verge of giving up, I decided to jump back a whole month to see if he ever did anything worth watching and something considerably more interesting appeared on his screen.

## ControlTest July 2052

Satellite images. Screens and screens of them. I watched my brother doing plenty of his own zooming and enhancing. He appeared to be looking at military grade imagery. Nemo was focused on photos of soldiers and of individuals in white coats with clipboards. They were all walking in and out of concrete complexes in some kind of mountainous region. Clipboards?

I looked at the timestamp on the images. 2032. Weird. I wondered why Nemo was looking at satellite pictures when we had better Panopticon coverage in Control, including high level drones. Our version of 2032 should be more complete than this satellite stuff.

On fast forward, I watched Nemo page through the imagery for the next two hours. I noticed he kept returning to one squat building. It seemed to be fed by a particularly high bandwidth stream of clipboards. I wondered what was going on in there. Presumably, so did Nemo.

Eventually, my brother pushed back his stool, picked up a sheaf of notes and maps from the table and slid them into a brown cardboard folder. On the front, in black marker pen he had hand drawn a map. His penmanship was appalling so I had no idea where it was supposed to be of. He looked at it and must have thought the same because he started rooting around for a felt tip. He picked one up and wrote in capitals on the cover: 'North Korea – 2032.'

# DRAGONS

## ControlTest July 2052

The rest of Nemo's week was spent immersed in the geography and geology of East Asia and in worldwide weather patterns in the early '30s. Then suddenly his video feeds switched to the bland fakes. He had clearly found what he was looking for and didn't want anyone else to know about it. He had something in mind for Utopia Five. What was it? The problem was North Korea didn't exist. It had never existed.

Some countries never adopted the Panopticon. North Korea was one of them. It presumably continues in its teetering state and we continue to have no idea what's going on there. Like the ex-tax havens, we haven't any data on the place and don't include it in any of the sims. If it were marked with anything it would be: 'Here Be Dragons'.

I needed to find out more about those concrete buildings Nemo had stared at so intently for hours. Assuming he hadn't become a fan of brutalist architecture, they must mean something.

Perhaps the imagery was in the public domain? I took some screenshots of the satellite photos and instructed Deus to correlate them with Korea and anything that happened in 2032. Twenty minutes later, the bot came back. It had found something.

According to Deus' search, the pictures Nemo was so engrossed by were from Omniscience's historical archive and were of a nuclear test complex. The site was on the far north east of the Korean peninsula, close to the Chinese border.

Cross-referencing the place with the date on the folder brought up an odd story in the memoirs of a North Korean physicist who'd defected to China after the Hot Summer. His book described an incident when he first arrived at the site in 2032. He realized that, for over 30 years, the technicians had been dumping low-risk waste material in a crevasse about five miles distant. He immediately stopped the practice and sealed the hole with concrete.

No records had been kept and no one had any idea how much potentially fissile material might have accumulated in there. The physicist joked the next bucket of rubbish emptied in could have hit critical mass and triggered the crevasse, test site, most of Korea and a chunk of China to disappear in a mushroom cloud.

I paused. It wasn't a great joke, but it was plausible.

In the 1980's, similar dumping had been discovered at a British nuclear research facility in the north of Scotland. I also vaguely remembered an incident from the Manhattan Project where a critical mass of fissile materials had accidentally been stored together in steel drums.

OK, I thought, this might have happened at every budding nuclear site. Humans liked to dump waste in convenient spots and a supercritical mass only needed fifty kilograms of uranium. Enough might accumulate in an unemptied rubbish bin over 30 years for the lot to go nuclear. It could work. It was a potential pivot.

This must be it. The story was classic Nemo. All he had to do was extract or distract one scientist – ensure he never plugged that hole – and he had a plausible source for the largest nuclear explosion ever experienced by mankind. I checked with Deus. A blast like that might have been multiple times the size of the Krakatoa eruption, which killed tens of thousands and darkened the sky globally for years.

This had Dystopia written all over it except for one thing. In order to destroy North Korea, he'd first have to add it to Control. Why would he create a whole country in the game only to immediately annihilate it? And I was confused. Wasn't this supposed to be a Utopia not a Dystopia?

I decided to see if there were any more clues on Nemo's untidy tabletop. I zoomed in and put the sim on fast forward. Something might show up. Pictures and pieces of paper moved around under Nemo's hands, appearing and disappearing before me until a fleeting image of a man's face caught my eye. I stopped and stepped back through the frames until it reappeared on my screen.

In front of me was a photograph I had seen only a day ago. The man who had been watching me through the Panopticon. Wigborough Wick.

# NEW ORDER

## *Analog 2037*

When the smoke finally cleared in 2037 and humanity was offered a future of more of the same by national governments, they did something they'd learned during the Hot Summer would keep them alive: they asked Deus what to do.

Kirby Cross was a thoughtful man. He took his responsibilities seriously. After everything that had happened in the past year, Deus had earned the faith of over five billion global inhabitants. That was most of us who were left. Those people had put their lives in its hands once. Now they wanted to do it again. Cross also had something even more powerful back then than trust: he had money.

In the long years when Kirby had been perfecting Deus, he'd had to tie together data feeds from hundreds of millions of drones and cameras. It took him until '29 to get it right. Later, I'd understand what a huge accomplishment that had been.

Nearly every major company in the world licensed Kirby's so-called OmniscientView for their own Panopticon products.  The View formed the basis of Omniscience Industries.

By the time Cross shipped Deus1 in 2030 it was just a marketing giveaway.  He was making his real money through data feeds to would-be competitors.  In 2037, Kirby realized the bot he'd launched as a sales gimmick was about to play a central role in deciding the future of humanity.

With an updated Deus5 chairing the discussion and Omniscience Industries bankrolling it, the largest coalition of individuals in history was formed.  The Panopticon supernation of five billion people began to thrash out a new world order.

# HELP

*Analog 2053*

Wigborough Wick! Who the hell was this guy? I pulled off my visor in frustration. I needed to talk through what I'd learned with someone else.

I now knew Laura and Ray were more than they appeared. After our encounter in the village of Furnace that afternoon, I'd checked the pair's social responsibility numbers. They were the highest I'd ever seen. I decided to take advantage of their apparently wise advice and climbed out of the van to look for them.

I finally found Ray pulling coins out of the ear of a giggling Sixpenny, who disappeared off with one when I arrived. I apologized for interrupting.

"What's on your mind?" he asked. I checked there were no drones around and told him everything I'd found out, including about the mysterious Wigborough Wick. During my tale, Laura came over from where she'd been talking to the drivers. When I finished, they looked at one another.

"I'd like to take a look at this world your brother Nemo created. This Utopia Five," said Laura. Ray nodded. "Is there any way I could do that?"

I was about to reply, "No, everything is offline," when a thought occurred to me. If they just wanted to look at the world, I had an option.

From my helmet's visor recordings, I downloaded the fifty hours I'd spent in Utopia Five before my access was cut off and sent it to them. Everything I'd seen or heard in the game they could review at their leisure. I hoped they'd spot something I hadn't.

"Thanks," said Ray. "Now, I have a suggestion for you. Your brother is good at hiding from the

Panopticon.  In fact, it sounds like he might be one of the best in the world at that particular trick."  I nodded, and Ray continued, "So don't look for him.  Search out this Wick guy instead.  He probably won't be as good at hiding his tracks and you might even find Nemo that way."

That was an excellent suggestion.  Nemo was world class sneaky.  Let's hope Wigborough Wick wasn't.

# ENEMY

*Analog 2053*

Well before dawn the next morning, I was awake and ready to start tracking down Wick. I needed to know who he was, what he wanted, and his connection to Nemo.

First, I had to stretch my legs and eat. I dug some leftover flapjacks out of the bottom of my bike panniers and clambered down from the truck. The drivers were sitting on a grassy bank by the side of the road, drinking mugs of steaming liquid from a kettle on a stove they'd obviously just set up. They called me to join them, and I shared my breakfast around in exchange for tea and information.

The three men knew one another of old. Their job was to drive specialists around the country for the Panopticon. "Wherever we're needed, we go," said one. "Which means wherever we go, we're needed," said the second. "And you can't ask for more than that!" chuckled the third man and they all laughed uproariously together. I wondered if they'd been drinking.

Cheerful as these guys were, I was unconvinced that was enough from life. There wasn't anyone who needed me except Nemo. I paused. 'Need' might not be the right word to describe how my brother felt about other people.

I wolfed down my breakfast then excused myself to resume my investigation. Back in the truck, I dropped my visor and fired up Deus along with my increasingly out-of-date copy of Control. Although the copy was too old to ID my bomber, it still had plenty of data to help me learn about Wick.

I considered what I knew about my target. I'd first noticed him two days previously, when Deus had flagged him as a persistent watcher of mine who'd been in the vicinity of my flat a few days before the explosion. That made him one of a thousand potential suspects.

I felt like I'd seen him somewhere before. Perhaps I'd glanced him around my flat? Having him show up in the Nemo investigations again confirmed my attention. As Auric Goldfinger said,

'Once is happenstance. Twice is coincidence. The third time it's enemy action.'

The Panopticon told me Wick's home was the city of Ipswich, north of London and not far from my brother's sprawling mansion. I'd initially suspected the bland persona was a cover. It wasn't. Until recently, Wick had been exactly what he said: a rural schoolteacher.

According to Deus, a year ago Wick was the organiser of a small group of beer-drinking friends who jokingly called themselves the Philosopher Kings. Their pub tirade was against the Panopticon's corrupting influence on free will.

Their main argument was, as we were observed all the time our behaviour was imposed on us. We couldn't choose our morality because we were coerced by the all-seeing-eye of the Panopticon to be good by society's definition, not our own.

Like Wick, most of his group were comfortable men in their forties. According to Deus, they'd been having this discussion in pubs across the region for two decades.  As far as I could tell, their hobby horse was harmless.  Then Nemo appeared.

The previous February, my brother had started showing up at their gatherings.  His sunglasses and trilby were enough to disguise him from the Panopticon but not me or Control.  We spotted him straight off.    Initially, he sat listening and occasionally asked how they felt, or what they'd done about it.  He fitted in well.  He had always had a slight anti-Panopticon leaning.

Nemo and I had debated the all-seeing-eye many times.  Crime was almost unheard of now. To me that's a good thing, but some people believe the Panopticon robbed us of our innate humanity.  I suspect if someone expressed their human nature by clonking Nemo on the head and nicking his wallet, he would be less than philosophical about it. He didn't see it that way.

The trouble was, Nemo was rich, clever, and articulate.  A convincing combination.  According to my recordings, he joined the Philosopher Kings every week and had long conversations with Wigborough Wick about why humanity loved the Panopticon.

They discussed how low crime wasn't even the main reason people wanted to be observed anymore. Everyone was used to that and expected it. Both men agreed we would keep it, even without the all-seeing-eye. "Humans no longer need to be watched to follow rules for the benefit of all," was Nemo's assertion. "To say otherwise is condescending. We can decide how to behave for ourselves!"

In their lengthy discussions, my brother and Wick ruled out zero crime as a factor that would make people battle for the Panopticon. I suspected they were right. People really did take a crime-free society for granted. They would assume it was unlosable, although I suspected they were quite incorrect about that. No, the two concluded what people loved, what they would fight for, was Deus.

Without the Omniscience bot, a lot more people would have died in the Hot Summer. That event changed how we saw ourselves and what we wanted our future to be. We had redefined society to include Deus and there was no Deus without the Panopticon. If you wanted to persuade people to sacrifice the all-seeing-eye, first you had to convince them to give up their new God.

"How might you get them to do that?" pressed my brother.

A few weeks later, Nemo asked Wick about his life before the Hot Summer.

He laughed, somewhat bitterly. "Back then I was a young hothead organising anti-Pan demonstrations, if you'd believe it. Of course, I was proved wrong. I might not like the all-seeing-eye but I'm not a fool. We wouldn't have made it through The Summer without it." He took a swig of beer. "But I would get rid of it *now*. We've learned our lesson. We put the WorldGov in place. *Now*, we don't need the Panopticon any more. It's holding us back."

"What do you think the world would look like without it?" asked Nemo.

"Free!" he replied.

# EXECUTION

## *Analog 2053*

We lurched to a stop so violently I was flung across my seat.

I had already unclasped my belt and was jumping down from the truck when Ray appeared looking breathless. "I need you. Come on," he panted.

He strode off with me behind. He beckoned Catterwade to follow. She had her visor down and a fleet of aggressive-looking drones hovering over her head. Laura and the kids were nowhere in sight. What was going on?

"I've been summoned as an undertaker," said Ray, sounding grim. "And I don't like the look of it."

He updated us as we walked. "I got a high urgency, direct command from the local mayor about 15 minutes ago as we passed this village." I looked at the grey housing around us, which was unprepossessing even in the bright sunshine. "Most of my calls are for elderly folk. This was for a 30-year-old man, so I did some checking."

"The guy is a farm labourer," he continued. "Bit of previous with drunk and disorderly but nothing major. This place is a phase 4 village. Very close to self-sufficiency. They'd had a request out for a judge to promote them to phase 5. They cancelled the judge at the same time they requested my services. That, I don't like. So, I'm taking you and Cat with me on this job. Just in case."

"Where are the others?" I asked.

"I've told them to lay low in the trucks, out of the way. They can watch through Cat's drones."

We strode into the main square. Like Furnace, this one was dry and dusty. On our left was a small town hall. On our right we could see the burned out remains of a huge agridome on what had, presumably, been the village green.

A crowd of angry, shouting people were gathered outside the dome. In front of the mob, a bewildered-looking man stooped with his hands tied together.  He had a black eye and split lip.  As we got closer, I could smell the alcohol on him.

"Looks like they've already given our guy a good going over," Ray commented.

A man I assumed was the mayor climbed onto a convenient crate and tried to calm the crowd. "This is a law-abiding village!  I know feelings are running high.  The dome was our lives, but we are not a lynch mob!  I've called the law!  Our undertaker has arrived!"  He pointed at Ray and the crowd turned to stare at us in expectation.

"It looks like they need a trial here," I whispered to Ray, "I didn't know you were a judge too."

"I'm not," Ray replied grimly.  "He didn't call for the law.  He called for me."

Ray stopped ten feet from the mayor and looked up at him.  Catterwade and I stood on either side with our visors down, scanning the crowd.  I wondered how offensive her drones were.

"Who has called on me, an executioner," Ray bellowed, "And why?"

It wasn't clear to me that "why" was part of Ray's job description.  I suspected that was Laura's role.  Ray was there to do the unpleasant stuff.  Nevertheless, the advantage of being a gigging executioner was you could choose not to take the work.  It was one of the benefits of freelancing.

"Look at what he did," the mayor spoke to us and gestured towards the smoking dome.  "We were only days off phase 5.  We've been working on it for years.  Last night we were woken up by the fire sirens, but it was too late.  Everything was gone."

The crowd became restless again.  A woman rushed forward and shoved the accused man to the ground.

The mayor continued, "We asked Deus who was to blame and it told us him!"  He pointed at the fallen prisoner.  "We went to his house.  He was drunk and asleep as usual.  By his bed we found this empty can of petrol."  He waved the jerry can around in an incendiary manner.

"Deus says he's guilty." He paused and looked around the crowd.  "We won't feed and house our own destruction!  Sabotage by arson is a capital offence. We call on you as an undertaker to execute him!"

It struck me the mayor wasn't calming things down.

I whispered to Ray, "This doesn't add up. You can't take an ID off Deus alone. It's easy to fool. No one would sentence someone to death without manually confirming it with Control. I guess Control hasn't been offline since '43 so that hasn't come up before. Maybe the mayor didn't realize?"

"Yeah, that's kind of why I brought you," Ray said, sotto voce, then continued more loudly, "This is a terrible crime." The crowd yelled in agreement. "So, I have brought *the* expert with me. The creator of Control, Lee Sands, will question Deus!"

He stepped back and looked at me. So did the big angry mob. Great. *Thanks for the oversell, Ray.* On the bright side, their pitchforks had presumably melted.

I connected to Deus and put the bot on my suit's speaker. We might as well start with the basics. "Deus, who set fire to the agridome? Was it that man?" I pointed at the accused who had been pulled to his feet.

"The evidence suggests yes," came the voice of God, which was designed to sound authoritative and succeeded.

"You see!" cried the mayor, mostly at the crowd.

"Probability?" I asked.

"96%."

"Based entirely on video evidence?"

"Correct."

That was fairly convincing. It was also massively overconfident. Deus didn't do imagery or subtlety that well. Why should it? It was a chatbot.

Omniscience had done a great job integrating the feeds from a billion drones and letting the whole thing be searchable. They didn't do detailed image processing or sophisticated probability assessment. They bought that from us.

Image analysis was what Nautilus did. Our interfaces were fully immersive visual experiences. Deus was a line of text and a speech converter. If Control was down, Deus shouldn't be letting people order groceries based on its own image recognition skills never mind sentencing folk to death. I was surprised the mayor didn't know that. Surely, he'd had some training?

I turned on my suit projector and threw a video up on the front of the village hall. It was time we took a look at this evidence. With only a bit of impatient shuffling, we watched the drone feed.

According to the timestamp, at 02:46 that morning a dark almost-silhouetted man in a cap and heavy coat had walked out of what Deus informed me was the accused's house. The figure was carrying a can of liquid. He checked his phone and then made his way to the agridome and walked inside. A few minutes later, it was alight and the fire alarms had triggered. I could see why a whipped-up mob would be convinced. The case looked open and shut.

"We can't make out the face of that person," I loudly observed. "Deus, what primary evidence did you use?"

"Clothing match 98%.  Location 95%."

Assuming the house was unlocked and the occupant dead drunk, I felt there were more options to consider.

"Deus, what if someone of a similar build slipped into the accused's unlocked house, picked up a hat and coat, and walked out wearing them? Would that also match the footage?"

"Yes, it would."

The crowd gasped at the experience of being presented with an alternative scenario.

I suppressed my frustration.  If Control had been online, I would just have run a gait analysis on the man in the recording.  Deus couldn't do anything that sophisticated.

I checked, but there was no further footage of the house.  All the town drones had then been diverted to fire suppression duties.  This three-minute video was all we had to go on.

"Surely the idea that someone else was involved is highly implausible," yelled the mayor.  "They couldn't know for definite that Deus hadn't recognized them!" The crowd nodded. It was a good point.

"Agreed," I replied. Then it struck me. Something I'd found odd about the recording had just been explained by the mayor. "You would want to check your disguise had worked before you broke the law."

I rewound and froze the projection at the point the figure looked at his phone. "I wonder what he was doing here. He was in the middle of committing a capital offence. I assume he wasn't checking the weather. Deus, please review your logs for ID lookups in this general area at," I checked the timestamp on the halted video, "2:47 this morning."

The voice of God responded, "According to my logs, I received a query at 02:47 for the identity of the individual in the currently displayed drone footage. I provided a 96% ID probability for the accused."

I mused aloud, "So, the prisoner logged in to confirm you absolutely knew it was him before he committed the crime. Or someone pretending to be him checked his disguise was successful before torching the building."

"Those are the two most likely options," responded Deus.

"Do you know who sent the query?" Ray interjected.

"No," replied Deus. "The source was withheld."

"Right folks," said Ray to the angry crowd who were looking slightly less sure of themselves. "I'm afraid you're going to have to hold a good old-fashioned trial before you string this guy up or you'll be the murderers. I'd recommend you gather all the evidence and call a judge. I'll check you do." He paused. "If I understand correctly, Control will be back online by the end of the week?" He looked at me.

I nodded. "Control will be able to confirm the ID of the arsonist from their walk and posture. That's better than clothes."

Ray continued, "After that, you can call a new undertaker. Until then," he added menacingly, "Don't waste any more of my time."

"But Control was offline when the crime occurred," said the desperate-looking Mayor. "We'll never know who did it!"

"Oh no, Control just inspects the data recorded by the Panopticon. That's all saved. We can look at it anytime once we're back up and running," I said. "Control won't have lost any data. As soon as I get the access sorted, you'll ID the perp no problem."

Ray turned on his heel and strode away from the bemused crowd before anyone could ask him to stay. Catterwade and I hurried beside him. The mayor was pale and oddly silent. He didn't call us back.

When we got back to the vans, Ray told the drivers to hightail it out of there as soon as possible. We didn't want to get delayed by Laura getting sucked into the trial. Not least because I clearly had to get Control back online fast.

"So," said Ray, "How did you enjoy your 'Twelve Angry Men' experience?"

"I assume it was the mayor?" I replied. As well as looking remarkably guilty he was a similar height to the poor schmuck he'd framed. "But why set fire to his own village? It makes no sense."

Catterwade snorted. "Oh, we've seen that happen before. It can turn nasty. That's why I brought the drones."

"A judicial Phase 5 review includes all the accounts," explained Ray. "I assume he's been cooking the village books. Those dodgy officials always get caught, but they often put up a fight. Burning the dome would probably put the review back six months for the cost of one measly life. He must have reckoned he could get the figures straight by them."

"Do you think he'll run?" I asked.

"Probably. If he makes it to North Korea before you get Control back online, he'll be home and dry." He laughed. "Otherwise," said Ray, "We'll send another undertaker after him. The next one won't be quite so genial."

# CRIME

*Analog 2053*

Back in my Control copy, I resumed following the relationship between my brother and Wick. Eventually, I pulled off my helmet and went in search of food.

I found Ray and Laura looking tired. Laura had to make another judge-stop and the caravan had only travelled 20 miles during the daylight.

I updated them on my investigations.

"So, you believe that while gathering background information for a computer game, your brother accidentally radicalized a mild-mannered schoolteacher?" Laura frowned. "He certainly does have a knack for the dystopian."

"Do you think Wick tried to blow you up?" asked Ray, cutting to the chase.

I replied, "I pulled up the direct Panopticon feeds of my flat for the day before the explosion. A delivery man carrying a heavy box walked into the building while I was out. Deus couldn't tell who it was. They'd disguised themselves like a pro. Wigborough Wick, however, is a plausible candidate. The build fitted."

I sighed. "Nautilus is so much better at image scanning than Deus. If I had Control, I could follow the delivery guy and identify him in a few minutes. Without it, a definite ID will take weeks."

I was conflicted. Wick looked increasingly like my bomber, but I was damned sure he didn't turn off my Nautilus access. There was no way he could've locked me out of my own machines. He was just a maths teacher. Nothing in his history implied hacking skills good enough to bar me from the system I'd helped design. Control being offline was still a mystery.

According to Ray and Laura, between halts that day they'd reviewed my trip recordings for Utopia

Five. I asked if they'd noticed anything that could explain what Nemo was up to.

"Utopia Five is a surprisingly unexciting sim," Laura replied. "We spoke to Sandy and he described some of your other Utopias and Dystopias. This one seems different. It is a dull world. However, in my opinion quite a believable one."

She continued, "The residents, denizens I believe you call them?" I nodded. "The denizens are remarkably unengaged in the society around them. Their lives seem to revolve almost entirely around killing time. It reminds me slightly of how people were at the start of the century. You don't tend to see that now. Outside of those individuals who have requested Ray's civic services, of course."

Ray nodded. "We focused on the last few hours you spent in the sim. The time leading up to your near miss with that gas canister." I cast my mind back to the rain and the depressing pub. Ray continued, "You noticed the barman robbed you?"

I froze in shock.

I must have looked stunned because Ray cheerfully elaborated. "You gave him twenty quid and he gave you change from a tenner. You didn't even notice. Just shoved the cash in your pocket without checking." Ray shook his head as if amazed at my behaving like such a mug.

In reality, of course, no one checks their change or expects to be conned in such an obvious way. The offender would be spotted, trivially, by the Panopticon and get a huge social de-merit. Casual crime doesn't pay. We don't even think about it anymore. Sophisticated stuff might be hidden for a while. It usually all comes out in the end.

It was impossible to grasp that I could be nicked from during an encounter in a Utopia. In a Dystopia, being short-changed would be the least of your worries.

I found the idea so unlikely I rudely flicked down my visor and fast forwarded my Utopia Five recording to the pub under the distressingly intact Big Ben. I reviewed my conversation with the barkeeper and paid close attention to my change. The greasy denizen had pocketed my ten quid without a qualm.

In the analog world, we hadn't had much visible crime since '35 when Omniscience Industries rolled out its 'Finger of Blame' app. It was the top download that year. Did they not have it in this world? That might mean the pivot pre-dated 2035.

I looked around the pub for the Panopticon cameras but couldn't see any. That was unusual for a public place. It wasn't illegal. It just meant your social score would be low. No wonder it was so empty.

I was still reeling at the blatant thievery when the television on the wall behind the bar caught my eye. I re-focused on that part of the recording. The star being interviewed on the bland celebrity chat show was Wigborough Wick.

# FREE WILL

*Analog 2053*

Re-tuning my visor to amplify the sound from the TV took me a moment. I could see Wigborough Wick was talking to a blonde anchor-woman in pink four-inch heels and matching lipstick.

He looked plumper than in real life and a lot more self-satisfied. His interviewer was asking about the disabling of the Panopticon in '36 and he replied it was about free will. "The right to choose our own destiny unwatched by Big Brother!" were his exact words.

This made no sense. Why would the denizens of Utopia Five turn off their best defense in the middle of the Hot Summer?

I raised my mask and turned to Ray. "I apologize. I did get thoroughly swizzed." He looked smug. "But did you see what was on the TV?"

Now it was my turn to feel superior as the pair looked at footage. "Bloody hell," said Ray. "That's a turn up."

We joined the others, who were eating by the largest truck, and brought them up to speed on what we'd learned.

They were intrigued by the theft. Petty crime had been wiped out by the Panopticon. Why was Utopia Five different? I remembered Ray's old business was "crime". I suspected he was ex-police, but it didn't matter. Even if he'd been a criminal kingpin, his social score was unquestionable now. Whichever way round, his history explained why he'd spotted the dodgy barkeeper and I hadn't. Maybe he had a better perspective on Nemo's so-called Utopia than me.

"Why does Wigborough Wick think people being able to steal would be a good thing?" asked the reliable Sandy.

"Well," replied Laura, "Some folk might argue that crime is an expression of free will. I could choose to take your sandwich while you were not looking." Sandy grasped his cheese roll to his chest. "Or I could decide not to," she continued. "If the Panopticon guarantees that I don't steal because I know I'll be caught, then I am no longer free to choose my own path. Even if you would be left to consume your supper unmolested."

Sandy looked skeptical. "Why should your freedom to choose trump my right to eat my dinner without it being nicked?"

That was the crux of Nemo and my arguments about the Panopticon. Freedom from crime gave people the chance to trust other folk and build society. I suspected that was more important than the freedom of an individual to make a bad choice. Nemo didn't agree.

The old Christian church believed people were only good if watched by an omnipresent deity. Our experience with the Panopticon proved that wasn't wrong. When everyone was observed all the time, they behaved pretty well. My brother reckoned this was only under duress therefore invalid.

He agreed that without the Panopticon many millions of people would have died in '36. But maybe, he suggested, millions would still die anyway. We hadn't had that much time with the Eye yet. Perhaps its observation would make humanity less willing to rock the boat and be creative. Then when the next disaster happened, we wouldn't survive it.

I could see Nemo's point, but why swap a good present for some Panopticonless future that might be better or could be much worse? Nemo did indeed have a knack for the dystopian. Maybe him disliking the Panopticon was the best argument for it.

"What about privacy?" said Ray. "In the old days you had the right to keep things secret about yourself. That's much harder now."

"Why would you want to keep secrets?" asked Tenpenny. "Unless you were doing bad things?"

Laura picked up the baton. "Sometimes people used to keep secrets to protect themselves from society. Perhaps their government had decided that people with red hair should be locked up. So, all the red-headed folk wore wigs in order that no one would know. That would be a secret."

"Why would a society decide something stupid like that?" questioned Tenpenny, scornfully.

"Clever people can be very persuasive," replied Laura.  "And everyone sometimes does things that are silly or dangerous.  Even governments."

"I don't think secrets are the right solution to that particular problem," drawled Catterwade.

I agreed.  Judging by the faces of the group around me so did most of us, but we'd had the Panopticon for nearly three decades.  I'd never lived without it.  Did we properly question it anymore?

Sandy looked worried.  "I still don't understand. Why does Wick hate the Panopticon enough to kill Lee?"

Laura looked at him kindly.  "You are right to question that.  Wick's concern is about something he clearly considers very important.  He fears people have lost the ability to choose right from wrong because the Panopticon forces them to behave how society wants, even if they don't want to act that way."

She went on, "Trust is fundamental to how things work now. We trusted and helped Lee even though we were strangers, and Lee trusts us. That wasn't so easy before the Panopticon. Anti–Pans worry that that trust isn't real. If you only rely on someone not stealing from you because they are constantly watched then they are not good, they are just supervised. Wick is worried that humanity has exchanged morality for observation or even coercion. A prison."

"That does sound bad," said Sandy. "What do you think?"

She thought for a moment. "I think Lee cares about Nemo because he is family. Family is a good basis for trust, but it doesn't scale. If we only trust people we know well enough to judge their character ourselves, that's limits it to a handful of folk."

She picked up her needles and started knitting. "An effective society uses every means possible to extend trust. I don't care how we do it. I don't mind why people are trustworthy as long as they are because I've seen what happens when we can't work together." Laura paused. "I suspect Nemo's Dystopias are useful. It's good to be reminded we live in a decent world but that we have to work at it. It isn't written into any rules it has to stay that way."

After the others went to bed, I stayed up with the drivers asking about what they'd seen outside the major cities. They told me more villages were becoming self-sufficient and more specialists like Ray and Laura were travelling around, helping maintain human networks of communication across the country. The drivers seemed optimistic about where this world was going. I hoped they were right.

Finally, I climbed into my usual truck. Before I went to sleep, I decided to check on Wick's current location. I instructed Deus to search for him in the Panopticon. He was nowhere to be found. Dammit. He must be hiding his identity. He could even be skulking around here. I asked Deus for the last known drone footage of him and it started to play inside my visor. I checked the time and location. Earlier that day, Wick had been in a car driving across the main bridge onto Angelsea. Through the window, I could see a person sitting next to him. I peered at the passenger, who was wrapped in a scarf and almost unrecognisable.

It was Nemo.

# ARRIVAL

## *Analog 2053*

The next morning, I wandered out looking for the others. Stone was using a pair of metal jugs to fill the wagon's microfilter tanks with water from a nearby stream. I strode over to help him.

I thought about what I'd learned the day before. It looked like we were all heading for the same place. A locus of people and circumstances was coming. I'd spent ten years studying events and I recognized a pivotal moment when I saw one. We were heading for a dangerous corner. A point from which things could get better or very much worse.

The trouble was my experience of dangerous corners suggested it was easier to screw things up than get them right. In the games, you were much more likely to create a Dystopia than a Utopia from a critical moment. That's why we called them dangerous. You were better off leaving them alone.

When we'd finished up, I left Stone and walked over to stand watching Ray cook pancakes. I needed to know more about Wick, I thought. I had no idea what he was planning other than my death. He had the strategic advantage. I was locked away from my tools and I didn't have the element of surprise. Unlike him and Nemo, I hadn't been hiding from the Panopticon. Wick knew I was coming and was presumably waiting for me. Angelsea was where my systems were. He knew I'd have to go there.

I needed a plan. I missed being able to talk my ideas through with my brother, but Ray and Laura were a surprisingly effective substitute. I'd never realized there were so many useful people out here in the analog world.

An hour later, I'd updated the pair on my thoughts and, while I ate the last of the pancakes, Laura laid out the key points as she saw them. "You don't know if Nemo is a prisoner; in the thrall of Wick; or if they are in league." She looked around to ensure we were paying attention. "In addition, you don't know what role Kirby Cross and

Omniscience Industries are playing. Are they on your side or Wick's?"

Laura had summed it up succinctly. I corrected her in one respect, "Nemo is an idiot sometimes, but he's not a criminal. He won't be in league with Wick."

Ray and Laura looked at one another.

Gently, Laura asked, "Were your parents killed during the Hot Summer?" I nodded and she continued, "Yes, we guessed you were brought up in one of the refuges."

She paused. "You know, that might explain Nemo's resentment of the Panopticon. It saved all those lives but did not save your family. Nemo is still young. I'm guessing Wick would be a similar age to your father. That may be influencing your brother without him realizing it."

I shook my head. "That isn't what Nemo is like. You'll understand when you meet him."

"Just bear it in mind," said Ray, forcefully. "So, you've told us you need access to your machines on the quiet, but they're in a secure Omniscience facility on Angelsea. D'you know anyone on the inside who could help you get in, no-one the wiser?"

I thought about the Omniscience Industries sales department. There were people I was friendly with. My gut told me they wouldn't stick their necks out for me.

I considered the engineers who looked after our kit. I'd worked closely with some of them. Again, I was pretty sure they'd help only up to a point. If I asked them to turn a blind eye to something dodgy, they'd shop me in a heartbeat, as Ray might say.

I reckoned I had to get onto the island, into our computing facility and physically in front of my machines. I needed to do that without Wick, Nemo or possibly Cross noticing, and Omniscience mustn't realize I'd lost access to the systems because that would raise alarms and get everything locked down until Nemo showed up. This was going to be tricky.

I'd last visited Angelsea a year ago to be sold on Omniscience's new private facilities. I'd ceremonially toured the building with the security chief. I remembered we'd got through the doors using an unduplicatable combination of my retinal scans. I'd been impressed and signed up. The

Heavenly Host worked well. It was secure. I didn't mind paying through the nose for it.

I thought about security. Someone had stopped me connecting to my systems remotely. If I had direct, physical contact with the machines, that would be different. Whoever it was, had they barred me physically from Omniscience? Or would my biometrics still get me inside?

We were a hundred miles from our destination in North Wales. We should get there late the next morning.

I had 18 hours to finish researching and an out-of-date copy of Control to do it with. I had to find out everything I could about Wigborough Wick and his friends. I needed to know what moves to anticipate.

At midnight, I flicked up my visor. It was going to be tough tomorrow and I'd need a few hours' sleep. First, however, I was aching and cramped from a day in the sim and I wanted a walk.

The truck was parked in a cleared area for the night. The sky was moonless with no light but the stars. I stared up at Andromeda and pondered who I was in this tale. I obviously believed I was the hero about to rescue Nemo. Was I kidding myself? What if I had everything the wrong way round? Maybe Wick was right, and I was the villain.

As I stood looking upwards, a figure stepped out of the darkness to join me.

"It feels like the eve of a battle," said Catterwade.

"Maybe more like the start of a war," I replied. "The trouble is I don't know what the war is about, who it's with or whether I'm on the right or the wrong side."

"You might not be on any side at all," Catterwade commented. "You may just be collateral damage."

I laughed. "That's comforting. For all I know, I might agree with the side that tried to blow me up and the best thing I could do would be to shoot myself." I paused. "Or become a line walker. End my old existence and do something new." We both fell silent for a long time, then Catterwade described her own life.

It was obvious the woman was a loner by nature. She told me she'd been a drone seeker since '36 because, back then, she'd wanted the solitude.

She talked about how tough it had been to start with. "The world was in chaos. I knew how to look after myself, though. That came in useful." She'd liked restoring fallen technology and contributing to the new society.

I'd noticed before she had a cool suit, so she obviously did OK.

Eventually, she'd realized she was missing something living alone with only broken drones and Deus to talk to. She'd run across the companions in '46 and they'd adopted her. The cart and shire horses were hers. The group used to travel around by truck. I found that surprising. Somehow the cart seemed more of a Ray and Laura thing. I asked if she knew how the two of them had met.

"I believe it was during the Summer. Laura and Ray were part of the official relief and rescue teams. It must have been harrowing. They both worked with the early City states and Deus to get things back on track. Then they left to travel and see what they'd built."

I thought about them both. I could see the value of folk like Laura and Ray – people who knew something about human nature before the Panopticon and understood how we could still behave when we weren't being watched.

# DISPLACED

## *Analog 2037*

Rolling up his bed mat, Nemo remarked, "I never want to see another church hall."

I could see his point. In the last year, we'd moved from one camp to another across the east of England. We'd slept in medical centres, tents, and occasionally a bed volunteered by a local. Mostly it was halls though. My new nightmares were about granite-like parquet flooring.

I finished unfolding a chair and a table, sat down, and fired up a lesson app on my phone. School was virtual. It kept going regardless of where we were. In that respect, school life was much the same as before. A key difference being we usually slept in our classroom.

"What's the status on our move request?" I asked.

Britain's major cities had escaped the Hot Summer relatively unscathed and that was where we'd decided to go. We'd decided the new city states had opportunities. We kept requesting transfers to London, claiming invented relatives who were keen to look after us. We reckoned once we got there, we could work out what to do next.

Nemo wandered back from the side of the hall where he'd put his bed away in a storage box.

"Deus says it's pending review," he replied glumly and sat down cross legged on the floor. "In other words, no change."

We'd soon realized the small refugee centres were full of people who didn't know what to do any more after their old lives had been wiped out. Losers. The ones who could handle the change made plans and didn't stay long. They moved on. I'd noticed the folk who'd given up sat and agonised endlessly about how things could have worked out differently for them if only they'd done some one thing. We swore we'd never to do that. Keep moving or die. Don't look back.

Nemo and I talked a lot about whether you could ever really alter fate. Either way, we wanted to be kinds of people who tried to change the future not the past and we didn't plan to stick around where we were.

I put down my phone. "The transfer's been 'pending review' for months. I'm sick of waiting. Does Deus know any way we can make this go faster?"

"I'll do some digging around," said Nemo, thoughtfully.

A month later we were still there. That was an unusually long time for Nemo and me to stay in the same location. Normally, some pleasant woman official would show up and move us to somewhere, "more suitable," which was usually indistinguishable from the last camp.

Four weeks had an unnerving feeling of permanence. The current hall was in the grounds of an old stately home and prefab dormitories had been installed there the previous week. We were imminently due to stop sleeping on the floor of the church and move into real beds in the new buildings.

The place wasn't bad. The staff were friendly and more unaccompanied kids arrived every day. I was peering in through the window of one of the chalets at what might be our future rooms when Nemo appeared behind me and coughed.

"They look OK," I said.

He nodded. "I've heard back from Deus."

I spun round. "What have you heard? Did we get our transfers?"

"Yes and no." He paused. "I worked out why we were never getting our requests approved. It was the relatives we made up. The system didn't recognise them. I tried but it's really hard to invent grownups the system will accept. There's no paper trail."

"Dammit!" I swore. "Do we have any other options?"

"It's hard to create adults," my brother said, grinning, "But it's not so tough to do a couple of kids. Most children look pretty much the same to the Panopticon. I managed it. Two transfers for 'Lee and Nemo Sands' with a friendly Uncle Oswald in London. We can go tomorrow. That is, if we want."

"Great. Let's go!" I stopped. "Hang on, won't this Oswald guy be a bit surprised to find out he has a couple of mysterious new relatives?"

"I've re-routed the alerts. He won't notice for months. By then, I'll have deleted our links to him again. He'll assume it was a weird glitch that someone fixed. There are plenty of them right now."

That was true.

"We can take the official transfer into London then sneak off. I'll update the system and we can turn up at a refugee centre as brand new orphans again. I've found one that looks good." As usual, my brother looked pleased with himself. "But are you sure you want to give up those nice rooms?" He pointed at the window I'd just been staring through. "The London centres are pretty crowded. This camp might turn out to be OK?"

"A bed would be nice, but this place is literally a mausoleum. There's nothing to do."

My brother laughed. "Keep moving or die?"

"Let's take off."  I agreed.

# ANGELSEA

## *Analog 2053*

The next morning, we arrived at our destination.

A huge grassy field had been cleared for specialists, many of whom were still arriving. Trucks were parked and tents pitched around the edges. A sophisticated array of solar panels, batteries and tables were set up with tools charging everywhere you looked.

An area at the centre of the field was covered and clearly devoted to humans rather than power generation. Ray dived off in that direction to find someone who knew the situation on the ground.

An energetic woman in overalls appeared. She informed us some kind of incident had taken place the day before that had partially broken the data flows for the area. There were rumours of an explosion on Angelsea. No evidence had yet appeared on the drone feeds and there was no word from Omniscience. Deus was still online, otherwise they would have gone in.

She continued, "The teams on site are routing around the Angelsea hubs. That seems to be unblocking the data. We reckon Omniscience is probably the source of the problem." She scowled. "The teams in the field are too busy getting data flowing again to start investigating the cause of the outages yet. That'll probably happen tomorrow."

A few minutes later, Ray returned. He was carrying a yellow dress and a large straw hat. "I've had an idea," he said.

Ray insisted we move our conversation into one of the lorries and disable the cameras.

"We've been thinking about how to make you less conspicuous for the next part of your plan,"

Ray said, looking pleased with himself. I regarded the bright, floor length kaftan and hat he had dug up. I didn't see how they would make me more discreet.

I'd been intending to hide from the Panopticon using a scarf, sunglasses, and cap. With Control offline, fooling Deus was comparatively easy. Control would have recognised me easily, but with my features covered, Deus and the Panopticon shouldn't spot me. As we'd seen in Ray's last undertaker gig, Deus wasn't that sophisticated at handling imagery. We really needed Control back.

"Yes, that would solve half the problem," insisted Ray, "But it would hide you from us. I have a better idea."

Ray had noticed a tall, well-built technician wearing rather eye-catching attire. His idea was she and I could go into a tent and swap clothes. The Panopticon would think I was her. If I kept the gear on, it would keep believing that.

"It should work. I reckon you're scrawny enough to wear the costume over your suit. Try it." He handed me the dress. "We can track her on Deus, and it'll show us you. She's happy to lie low for the day and you'll look like you're still somewhere in the camp. As long as you keep your face out of view, the Panopticon and Deus won't spot you."

I'd hoped my first covert operation would be more James Bond and less pantomime dame. Control would never be fooled by such an obvious trick, but hopefully Deus would. The best thing was Nemo would never think of it.

A few hours later I was standing at a small boat club. As usual, the sky was blue and the sun hot. I looked across the channel at my island destination.

I'd decided crossing by one of the bridges would be too obvious. They were closely monitored, and my disguise wouldn't withstand a human watching a direct feed. There was, however, a constant stream of vessels taking day trippers to the island. The place was the private property of Omniscience but had good beaches and they turned a blind eye to trespassing sunbathers. That was my way in.

I had felt uneasy as I'd left my usual ride at the camp and borrowed a jeep to drive to the sea, but I'd had no choice. The bike would have been too recognisable. Leaning against one of our trucks, it supported the story I was still around.

My plan was to hire a boat at the sailing club. That would take me close to my target. From there, it would be up to me to get into the secure facility.

If the captain of the launch thought it odd I was wearing a voluminous, banana-coloured kaftan over a full body haptic suit with knee high military boots, he didn't mention it. I'd hidden the helmet and gloves in my huge rucksack. No one comments on you taking enough stuff to a beach to mount a small military invasion. As long as you've got a parasol.

On the other side, I waved my thanks, jumped down onto the sand, and walked up the shore towards a thicket of trees. I was safely on the island. Now for the next stage.

I set up the parasol and a windbreak against the edge of the copse and disappeared into my makeshift tent. Away from the eyes of the overhead drones, I pulled off the dress, put on a cap and sunglasses, and crawled into the adjacent shrubbery.  It was dense enough to hide me from overhead cameras.

A quarter of a mile and a few scratches later, I emerged onto the side of the road.  Without Control, the Panopticon wouldn't recognize a location move of that distance combined with an extreme clothing change.  I strolled to the nearest bar and looked at my watch.  I had three hours.

# GUARDIANS

## *Analog 2053*

"Jeff! It's Lee Sands... Indeed, it has. I'm in the area and decided to drop by and check on my assets. I'm thinking about doubling the capacity and I'd like to see how the security upgrades are going. Why don't you pick me up and give me a tour?... Haha!... About a mile away... How about right now? Great Jeff, I can always rely on your fast response." I hung up.

That would give my keenest account manager little time to report to anyone I was on the island. Four minutes later, Jeff breathlessly arrived in an electric buggy. He appeared overcome with excitement.  Salesmen were predictably coin-operated.

If Jeff single-handedly closed me on doubling my spend, he'd pocket more money in commission than he might otherwise see in his career.  He was going to do a great deal to keep me happy.  I just needed to maintain the dollar signs in his eyes.

We arrived at the hosting complex in Jeff's vehicle, were waved straight through the gates and up to the front doors, and got out and walked in.  Easy.  Now for the theatrical part.  I could see the salesman was itching to take me to a meeting room and give me a lengthy presentation.  That wasn't quite what I had in mind.  I asked to see the head of building security.

"Dave," I said, when the tall man appeared.  "Great to see you again.  How are the kids? Fantastic.  I don't have much time."  I checked the patently expensive watch I relied on for such meetings.  "You know what I'd love to look at?  The current security.  Let's re-validate against my biometrics."

We tested out the systems while he described the building's enhanced security hardware and I nodded sagely.  I checked the planned install dates on their new MRI-based IDs and got him to show me the prototypes and give me a demonstration.

I joked I'd have to come back and update my biometrics, or I wouldn't get into the building myself. They both laughed too heartily, especially Jeff, but I could see the charms of my cheque book weren't lost on the security head either. We inspected all the entrances. I asked tough but perceptive questions and made impressed noises. In other words, I laid it on thick.

After an hour, Jeff and Dave looked like men about to explode with the anticipation of a highly lucrative deal and the desire not to screw it up. By the time we got to the servers, they didn't turn a hair when I connected my suit to one of the worker machines. "Good," I said. "The individual machines also enforce biometrics. I wondered if you'd completed that upgrade."

I turned to Dave. "This is a state-of-the-art facility," I declared and gave him the kind of approving smile a security chief would treasure all his life.

Jeff drove me back to the bar. I turned down his offer of drinks. "Love to, Jeff. Love to. But friends waiting."

As we parted I shook him by the hand, deliberately re-exposing the watch. I put my other hand on his arm and looked deep into his eyes. "Jeff," I said, "I could not be happier with this visit. Call me Monday with some quotes."

As he drove off, I knew he wouldn't log this meeting for at least a week in case his boss "re-assigned" the commission. There was no honour amongst salesmen. That was part of their culture. They seemed to be happy with it, so the Panopticon hadn't made any difference.

The head of security would be unlikely to report the visit either. The occasional surprise spot check from an arsehole CEO was business as usual. It should be days before anyone else found out I'd been in the facility. If I survived until Monday, I'd order a hefty chunk of new kit in gratitude to my inadvertent inside men.

I left the bar. It was starting to fill up with locals I assumed were Omniscience employees because my haptic suit didn't stand out. I strolled back into the trees then crawled through the undergrowth to my beach tent. I changed back into my loud outfit and emerged 2 hours and 45 minutes after I'd entered my makeshift hide. It was 15 minutes before my returning boat.

Two hours later, I was back at the camp. As far as Deus and the Panopticon were concerned, Lee Sands had never left.

# CONTROL

*Analog 2053*

It was sunset.　The others had spent the day helping with the re-routing efforts.

"How did it go at Omniscience?" asked Ray.

"Perfectly," I replied. "I got everything I needed and with any luck my visit will stay secret. No one should realise what I've done."

I was tired, but I still had a lot to do. Tonight, I would visit Omniscience Industries more formally. Nemo had already been in there too long and I needed to go in after him. I'd have to complete my preparations that evening.

My fleeting connection to the machine in the server racks had been the point of my trip. It had taken my suit 138 milliseconds to download the entirety of Utopia Five and Control. I now had everything I needed. I could start answering some questions.

I sat on the grass with my back to the truck, pulled down my visor and loaded a fully up-to-date Control. God, how I'd missed it.

As I'd explained to the angry mob only the day before, Control was what really watched over us. It did most of the image processing for Omniscience. Deus and the Panopticon were easy to fool. Control would never have been deceived by my charade with the dress. With Control out of action, the Panopticon was a lot less effective. For the past four days, without an up-to-date version I'd been blind.

## Control, 2053, 5 Days Previously

I stood invisibly on my street, watching a delivery man drive up to my flat, park, and carry a heavy box inside. He left after twenty minutes. I followed him as he drove off and returned his hired van. At the nearest train station, he disappeared into a public toilet and emerged in a different coat with his hat and scarf removed. He caught the next train to Ipswich.

## Control, 2053, 4 Days Previously

In the same street, I waited in front of my house again. Suddenly, a figure in black leapt from a first-floor window, landed nimbly on the road in front of me and started running.

A second later, my house exploded. As chunks of masonry landed around and through my avatar, I pondered that, on the positive side, I hadn't just cleaned the flat because that would've been doubly annoying.  Although, perhaps if I'd been a bit more assiduous about housework, I would have found the bomb.  There was a lesson there.

I rewound the scene until my denizen jumped backwards through the open window into my ex-lounge and then I froze the playback.  That must have been the point I'd noticed someone observing me in Utopia Five.  The analog, real world time stamp was 14:34:36.

I brought up my recently acquired Utopia Five game logs.  At 14:34 there were only two players logged in.  The first was me.  The second was my mysterious watcher.  His user ID was WWick.

In Control, I jaunted to Wick's home in Ipswich and replayed the same time.

Two minutes after the explosion, he staggered out of his house looking shaken.  He must have been watching through a drone feed, seen me escape and realised what his failure to kill me in that blast would cost him.  Alive, I could track him down in minutes.

He tapped a conspicuous bulge in his jacket pocket, which I assumed was a gun rather than a handy snack. He peered up and down the street as if amazed police cars weren't already arriving to arrest him, then looked at his phone.

I hazarded he was checking where I was. He gazed at the screen in his hand in relief. I guessed he had seen Control was down. It was a reprieve! Even if it was temporary? He made a quick call, then grabbed a bike that was leaning on the side wall and cycled wildly to a pub a few miles away. When he got there, he went inside and flopped down with a pint. He stared at it as if wondering if it would be his last.

My invisible avatar stood and waited. Twenty minutes later, my brother arrived.

# HOT SUMMER

*Analog 2036*

Even I knew we should've seen what was coming a whole lot sooner, and I was only 11.

We were all aware summers had been getting progressively hotter for years, and storms and wildfires were bigger. Almost everyone agreed it was a problem and they talked about it endlessly on the TV and in the newspapers. The government even did some stuff, but it was just never quite enough. In '36 we were finally woken up. Unfortunately, by then we only had six months.

The summer of late 2035 in the southern hemisphere was the hottest and driest on record. That wasn't a surprise. It was true of most new summers. I'd always loved the weather, we could be splashing in the sea or playing on the beach almost all year round.

2036 started differently. In January, when Tasmania began burning, I remember we were shocked. Hundreds of thousands tried to evacuate, and the scale of the destruction was beyond belief. Nemo wasn't allowed to watch the vid feeds; he was too young.

A few weeks later it was the turn of eastern Australia. Even then, back at home we didn't see the implications. I remember thinking Australia was a long way away and it was always hot. It didn't really sink in until New Zealand. At that point, we finally grokked what was happening.

In the northern hemisphere, we cut down woods and forests in panic. The TV showed people razing parks and gardens. Even I joined the gangs digging and clearing ditches. I helped build fire breaks and watched men burn off scrubland as fast as they could. We did everything possible to protect people, buildings, and crops.

A cloud of smoke rose above Europe, Asia and North America. Was the great felling a good idea? Probably not. We were buying problems for tomorrow, but people were frightened today, and we didn't have time for a debate. We'd only need to worry about what happened next if we survived the Summer.

Britain used the Panopticon. The nation turned over our giant drone army to the war against Summer. For over a decade, the world had been using small UAVs fitted with IR scopes and chemical extinguishers in firefighting. They were highly effective. They suppressed conflagrations as fast as inhumanly possible, and that was quick. We diverted all the Panopticon drones blanketing our cities to the flying fire watch.

Everything in the air joined the battle to fight the coming heat. At home, we installed new software and contributed our private fleet to the effort – we had three security drones and they were good ones. Nemo obsessed over the fire feeds. The rest of us dug bore holes for water, pored over official warning guides, and got ready as best we could.

The government banned smoking, matches, fires, even glass bottles. Everything was enforced by the Panopticon's giant hovering eye and millions of human ones, including me and Nemo, glued to cameras. We watched for the slightest spark.

It wasn't enough. By the end of the year, hundreds of thousands were dead in Europe alone from fires and storms. Millions more were starving or homeless. Humanity had been decimated. We were lost and frightened and, inexorably, summer would be coming again.

Ironically, our darkened sky bought us a reprieve. 2037 was cold and wet. Global dimming from the fires had given us a few years. We all understood that when the ash finally cleared, things could get even worse.

Our governments and corporations immediately started encouraging people to return to their old lives as if they'd learned nothing. So they might have done. If it wasn't for God.

By the late 20's, the Panopticon's army of observers had been incredibly effective at reducing crime in Britain. As a result, the concept had quickly been embraced and adopted by most of the developed world.

When I was growing up, the idea of being robbed never occurred to me. No one locked their doors and we all wandered straight into our friend's houses with nothing but a loud yell to announce our arrival. I still find it bizarre that wasn't true before the all-seeing-eye of the Panopticon.

Kirby Cross' Omniscience Industries rode the expansion of the drone cloud and his Deus chatbot continued to be the most popular way to access the all-seeing-eye. Omniscience became one of the most successful companies on the planet.

For Nemo and me, Cross and Deus felt omnipresent during the hurried preparations for the Hot Summer. In May '36, Omniscience Industries helped with the war effort by rolling out Deus4. The new bot gave users access to fire cameras, knowledge of local preparations, weather alerts, and excellent advice based on data unparalleled in human history.

Deus was Nemo's constant companion. I think he talked to it more than he talked to me, and it was my job to stick to my little brother like glue. In retrospect, I wondered if that was how he and I got out.

Unsurprisingly, Deus4 picked up the nickname "God". Omniscience never did manage to get the trademark.

# CHANGE

## *Control 2053*

"Hi Wigborough! What's up?" Nemo said cheerfully, taking off his hat. "I'm glad you called. I need a favour. I have to lay low for a few days. Lee will be looking for me and I've got to stay well out of the way. I was thinking we could take a road trip?"

Wigborough Wick looked nonplussed. "Is this anything to do with Control being down?"

"Completely," continued Nemo. "I disabled all access to it." He checked his watch. "About half an hour ago. Lee can't get in and neither can anyone else."

Wick looked like a man with an unexpected and miraculous reprieve.  Nemo looked oblivious.

"But why?" asked Wick.

"I need Lee to think properly about Utopia Five without any distractions."  Nemo took a gulp of his pint.  "The people in the game are strange.  I don't understand them.  Lee is way better at that stuff than me.  Much more likely to get to the bottom of it."

"My work-obsessed sibling is going to go crazy," Nemo continued, laughing, "But we both spend way too much time online.  We should be out there, shaking up the real world.  Changing things.  Just like you and I want to do.  U5 will get everyone really thinking and talking about the choices we've made.  It'll be great when we launch it, but I want Lee's thoughts on how to do that."

Wick had a strange expression.  "I suspect you're right about the game," he said, "it would definitely shake people."

"So, I decided to lock the work servers for a few days and sneak off and stay with you, if you'll have me?"

Wick nodded as if he was thinking about something else.

"That'll force Lee to de-helmet and concentrate on reality for a change. Maybe even meet some actual people not just denizens." Nemo paused in reflection. "Trying to get Lee to do that was why I moved out of the flat. It didn't work all that well, but I reckon this time will do the trick."

"So, what will happen now?" asked Wick, absentmindedly tapping his jacket pocket.

"It won't be easy to find me with Control offline. Lee will probably have to cycle to the physical servers in Angelsea to get things back. That'll take a few days. Loads of thinking time."

Wick looked thoughtful. "Why don't we head in that direction ourselves? Meet Lee there?"

"Good plan!" said my brother. "We can visit Kirby and I can introduce them."

"That sounds ideal," replied Wick.

# TWO WORLDS

*Analog 2053*

That explained my systems lockout.

I flipped up my visor. Damn Nemo! If I'd had access to Control, I could have IDed Wick as the bomber, had him arrested by Mrs Lewis and her librarians, and closed out the whole issue inside 24 hours. Everything would have been easy!

Wick must have relied on taking me out so I couldn't use my own systems to find him. I guess that showed, when you come at the administrator you'd better not miss.

He'd only got away with it because Nemo had disabled my access. My brother's unfortunately timed decision to stage an intervention on my social life might yet kill us both.

My Control visit had answered some of my questions, but I still didn't know what Wick wanted or why he'd tried to kill me. Everything was pointing me back to Nemo's decision to create his own Utopia. Why had he decided to do it? That had started all of this off. The answer to what Wick wanted must be in that world and I had to find it.

I needed to return to Utopia Five.

## Utopia Five, 2053

Standing in front of Big Ben, it was still cold and raining. Damn, I should have remembered to appear inside. In the real Britain, it never drizzled. It was either hammering with rain or baking hot. You might think a shower would be a nice change. You'd be wrong.

I re-entered my dreary pub four days after I'd left it. Game time had kept pace with the real world. I could have returned just after I'd gone, but there wouldn't have been any point. The system had already forgotten my earlier presence. Visitors didn't affect a sim world for more than a day unless they paid for a pivot.

I stormed up to the bar with cold water trickling down the back of my neck again. I still didn't know why they added that feature to the suits. My thunderous approach terminated with me grabbing the barman by the front of his leather jacket. My Eloi avatar was quite big.

"Hold on mate!" he yelled, "It was only a fricking tenner!"

His response distracted me both from punching him and my damp collar. Firstly, since the system couldn't have remembered me, that was a good guess by our denizen. It implied a repeated offence. Secondly, in my opinion stealing was a binary decision. You either nicked stuff or you didn't. To our bartender here crime was clearly more of a spectrum. That must make moral judgements difficult.

"When I was in here before, there was a guy on the TV talking about the Panopticon," I demanded. "Wigborough Wick. Do you know anything about him?"

The barman looked blank. "The Panopticon," he squeaked, "What's that then?"

The sleazy criminal I currently had by the lapels was an uninspiring denizen. Nonetheless, from what I'd seen he was representative of the people in this world. It looked like Nemo had succeeded both in turning the Panopticon off and in wiping all knowledge of it from a reasonable proportion of the population. The question remained, how had he done it?

I appeared to have reached a dead end in this sim once more. This time, however, I had no mysterious watcher to distract me. I intended to finish what I'd started when I got here before. I would go and have a long chat with Lee Sands.

I re-materialized on my own street. This time, I'd had the sense to give my avatar an umbrella and I could hear rain beating against it.

A terrace of grey stone townhouses stood before me, and I stared at one. In the real world, it was my now-flattened home. In Utopia Five, the building was still standing, and the Victorian road it was on looked much as it had done before the current events. One difference was there were huge plane trees lining it. In my world, street trees hadn't survived the pre-Summer panic felling. Our re-planted ones were a lot smaller.

In most of the Nautilus worlds, if this house existed then I still lived in it. The games engine used our real behaviour to deduce our denizens'. If I hadn't moved in ten years, why would any of them?

My avatar walked up to the nameplate on the front door. It confirmed Lee Sands lived here. Nemo and I clearly hadn't bought the place in this world as there appeared to be six flats. I rang the bell, waited and after a few minutes the door was answered by a slight, short haired individual in their late twenties, wearing a thin pair of jeans and a sweatshirt.

I paused for a moment.  "Hello Lee," I said, "I'm you."

Lots of players think denizens are real. Although, when they upgrade to premium, they seem happy to shoot them.  I try not to think too hard about that.

Denizens are not people.  They just feel like it because that's entertainment.  Nautilus generates the behavioural algorithms for all of them.  There's no magic.  It's statistics, not metaphysics.

I'd never broken Nemo's second commandment: "The Denizens are Sacrosanct".  I had never reprogrammed one to do what I wanted. Programming, however, wasn't the only way they learned.  Just because I didn't cheat didn't mean I'd never bent the rules.

In the analog world, every three months for the past ten years I'd paid a different actor to turn up at my front door and say, "Hello Lee, I'm you."

The Panopticon would watch the real me take the rent-a-me upstairs, hand them a cup of tea, and spend the next hour giving them a thorough presentation on modern history since 2025. None of the people I'd hired had ever questioned it. I suspected they got worse gigs.

The result was in every Utopia and Dystopia Lee Sands had a flat full of photos of world leaders and, if asked in the right way, would happily provide you with an excellent synopsis of world events since the Panopticon. As far as the Nautilus algorithms were concerned, exposition was my hobby.

Five minutes after knocking on Lee Sands' door in Utopia Five my avatar was sitting on a camp chair in a dilapidated front room sipping tea while my denizen filled me in on the world.

# UTOPIA FIVE

*Analog 2053*

It was midnight in the real world, and everyone was waiting to hear what I'd discovered on my final trip to Utopia Five. We'd already accumulated a crowd of people who wanted to know why the camp was buzzing about break-ins at Omniscience Industries. The time for secrecy had clearly passed.

That afternoon, before I'd re-entered Utopia Five, I'd installed a copy on one of the camp servers. I'd decided, if the game was so controversial, I should let as many people as possible see it. Our fans worldwide had leapt at the chance to play for free. I was resigned to the fact we were never going to make money on it anyway.

I stood in a clearing at the centre of the assembled mob. A cloud of drones buzzed around overhead. Some were Panopticon, some private. I could see several of Catterwade's.

After the explosion earlier in the week and the Utopia Five release today, I had a lot of viewers. I checked. It looked like around 109 million were watching worldwide. I reckoned more would catch up the next day. I cleared my throat and waited for the crowd to quieten down.

"My name is Lee Sands," I shouted. "This week, my home was destroyed, and an attempt was made to kill me."

There was nodding from the crowd. The Panopticon footage of me leaping out of a first-floor window with a building exploding behind me had become an internet hit.

"Today, many of you played our new game. I believe it holds the key to why someone wants to silence me."

There were more nods from the gathering.

"I think my brother created Utopia Five to see what the world would be like with no Panopticon."

There      was      a      collective      gasp.

# THE CASTLE

## *Analog 2053*

At 4 a.m., I left the camp. I couldn't wait any longer. Nemo had been on Angelsea with Wick for too long already. According to the Panopticon, they had strolled into the Omniscience HQ together and never come out.

I told Ray and Laura I was going there alone. This was my fight. The problem had been created by my games and my brother and I needed to fix it. I turned on my IR sensors and cycled across the iron bridge in the dark. There wasn't a soul on the roads. No one challenged me.

The famous HQ of Kirby Cross' company was a huge stone keep on the eastern shore of the island. Beaumaris Castle was certainly beautiful. Kirby had apparently fallen in love with it and sworn to save it from the rising sea.

The place had been built by an English king 800 years ago then miraculously bypassed by all conflict, leaving it oddly pristine. Through my infrared scope it loomed pale green, unworldly, and perfect. It was like something out of a fairy tale, and I wondered if someone was going to come to a gruesome end there. I hoped it wasn't me.

Cross had added to the unreality by having it enclosed in the largest glass dome ever built. I suspected it was meant to symbolize the wealth and power of Deus. A new Wonder of the World. A critic might mention it looked like a giant snow globe.

Nemo loved it.

In Control, I'd watched Wick and my brother arrive and walk in through the gates. The place had been buzzing with people. After all, it was the centre of operations for the largest remaining global enterprise. In the middle of the night, it was deserted.

I left my bike and walked up to a pair of huge doors in the colossal dome. They swung open. Like everywhere in the real world, nothing was locked.

Inside the hemisphere, the building and grounds were dark as well as empty. Omniscience clearly observed the blackout. It was also silent except for a single Panopticon drone, which buzzed over my head. Someone would know I was coming. Was that a friend or foe?

With my night vision enabled, I crept along a stone path and across a perfectly manicured lawn towards the southernmost gatehouse. On my last visit, a castle guide had shown me its murder-holes: slots in the walls for dumping boiling oil on unwelcome visitors. I hoped Wick hadn't had the same tour. I extended my prox detectors and prayed he wasn't about to go medieval on my ass. *Thank Deus he's not a history teacher.*

I approached the tower tentatively. My sensors gave me the all clear, and I jogged through. On the other side, the middle of the keep lay in front of me. It was a grassy area full of trees and, almost hidden amongst them, I could see a small figure. I increased my visor magnification.

It was Nemo.

"What the frack are you playing at?" I swore as we hurried down a stone passageway on the north side of the keep.

Nemo ignored me. "What took you so long?" he asked. "We're all below decks. We've been waiting for you to get here."

I'd been to Omniscience before, and I knew the setup. Impressive as the castle was, it was hardly sufficient for the largest multinational in the solar system, even if Earth was poorer than it used to be, and the Mars and Moon bases were only research stations.

Beaumaris Castle was the tip of an industrial iceberg. It rested on a subterranean complex that stretched over a kilometre north and west and 100 metres down. Underground, it was big enough to house all the Omniscience staff and many of their servers in a style that would survive a category 8 hurricane.

The tunneling tech humanity had developed for the new off-planet colonies had proved useful at home. Most major cities had underground shelters. Omniscience's was just unusually extensive. A bad enough variant of one of our modern storms would have blown the medieval keep away like a toy. In reality, their insurers would never allow an above ground HQ.

The lifts down were in the northwest tower. That appeared to be where we were heading. "What are we running towards?" I asked.

"We're all downstairs," Nemo replied. "We've been keeping Wigborough happy until you arrived. I wish you'd got here sooner. I'm starting to wonder if bringing him here was a mistake." He paused. "He's behaving oddly, and Kirby is worried. You might need to sort things out. I'm sure he's harmless, though."

Nemo's expression made me doubt the truth of that statement. I needed to get down there.

The lift doors were standing open when we arrived. My brother started to rush in, and I grabbed him by his collar and pulled him back out. Wick was a fan of DIY explosives and had been here for some time.

I insisted we walk down the emergency stairs. They were solid and bare. I was confident Wick couldn't have hidden any booby-traps in there.

"Aren't you being a bit paranoid?" asked Nemo. He seemed amused.

When we reached an exit marked seven, my brother stopped. "This is Kirby's level."

I sent him down another two flights, pulled down my visor and tentatively stepped through the door. I emerged into a wide corridor stretching left and right with doors on each side every 20 feet. The corridor curved out of sight in both directions.

"You are in a maze of twisty passages," I murmured to myself.

It was painted sky blue with white clouds. It wasn't what I was expecting, but I'd never visited this level before. Most of the public offices were on one.

"Come on!" shouted my brother. He dodged around me, dashed down the corridor, and dived into a room around 30 feet away.

*Dammit Nemo!* I gritted my teeth, kept my visor down, and followed him.

When I walked into the room, I was confronted by the sight of a man in his eighties slumped in an armchair. He was dressed in a long white gown and a gently glowing holographic halo floated over his head.

Kirby Cross was clearly a CEO who drank his own Kool Aid, I thought. I was impressed he'd maintained his brand during what was, presumably, a hostage situation.

He sat up when Nemo rushed in. "You found Lee!" he exclaimed. "Thank goodness. Now perhaps your friend will calm down and we can finally go to bed," he said in a relieved tone and flopped back into his seat.

I'd never met Kirby Cross before, but I knew he and Nemo had played D&D together for years. I looked around. His sitting room was dimly lit, which I assumed was to show off the halo. The place was empty except for Kirby, Nemo, and a mousy-looking man in his late seventies who felt familiar.

I checked the new visor programming I'd finished the day before. It confirmed I'd seen him with the Philosopher Kings at one of their early meetings. It appeared Wigborough Wick wasn't entirely alone. The man, however, didn't look like a guard. He seemed as uncomfortable as Kirby.

"Wigborough is outside," said Nemo, answering my unspoken question.

I looked incredulously at my brother and Cross. "Have you been sitting in here waiting for me to arrive, without doing anything about being kidnapped?" I demanded.

"Kidnapped? What on earth are you talking about?" Nemo stared at me. "Wigborough wanted to visit, and I hadn't seen Kirby in a while. Plus, I needed to dodge you for a few days. So, we came here." He addressed his final comment to Cross. "We're just on holiday."

Nemo continued, turning back to me and laughing nervously, "I'll admit Wigborough got a bit worked up after he played Utopia Five and he has been acting strangely since then." He paused. "So, I thought it might be a good idea to wait for you to arrive and find out what's the matter. You're good at that sort of thing." Nemo looked apologetic. "I fiddled with the Welsh data lines to hurry you up, but I could see you were already on your way." He hesitated. "Wigborough is harmless," he added again.

"Harmless!" I hissed, furious at my little brother. "He's a maniac! He blew up our flat! He thought I was in it!"

Nemo looked horrified, but also guilty. He'd clearly suspected he was underplaying things and hadn't wanted to admit it. "Something happened to the flat? Why didn't anything warn me?"

"Because you're in hiding, you idiot! And keep your voice down," I whispered angrily. "He could be back any moment!" I thought how bizarre it was that Nemo could spend his whole life dreaming up ways everything could go to hell and still fail to spot it happening in front of him.

Kirby looked stunned. "I thought your friend was an odd chap, but why on earth would he want to kill Lee? I don't believe it." He turned toward me. "Are you sure you haven't misunderstood things? Perhaps we should discuss it with him when he gets back?"

*I suspect I'm not the only one he wants to kill*, I thought. They had no idea of the danger we were all in.

I'd need to talk fast.

# PIVOT

*Analog 2053*

Earlier that day, my denizen had filled me in on the world of Utopia Five. It appeared Nemo really had managed to bring about a society without the all-seeing-eye.

As I knew from my trips to Control, it had taken him months of research into the early Panopticon. How it worked, how it could be disabled and, most importantly, how people might be persuaded to turn it off.

In 2036, Deus and the Panopticon had saved humanity. After that, we would never choose to live without them. If Nemo was going to get rid of them, he'd have to create a world where the Hot Summer had never happened.

In his primary Utopia Five pivot in 2034, the mysterious suicide of a physicist ultimately resulted in a massive incident at a North Korean nuclear facility. The explosion blasted half of the country and a significant chunk of southern China into the atmosphere.

Before his change, Nemo had spent weeks reading about the greatest volcanic disasters recorded by mankind. On 10th April 1815, Mount Tambora in the Dutch East Indies erupted. It was the largest explosion on Earth in nearly 2 millennia. It had belched ash into the air for three years and the debris darkened the sky across the world. 1816 was known as the 'Year without a Summer'. Extreme weather patterns and failed harvests spread across the globe.

In 1883, the East Indies was hit again. Mount Krakatoa exploded with 13 thousand times the power of the Hiroshima nuke. This time, global temperatures fell by over a degree. They didn't return to normal for five years.

That was the core of my brother's plan.

In Utopia Five, Nemo's nuclear accident caused dimming ash to settle over the planet. Cold, grey mist enveloped humanity. His geoengineering averted the Hot Summer or at least, according to his calculations, delayed it for decades.

In their version of 2036, the most urgent issue was growing food in the reduced sunlight. As the dark world reeled and tried to grow enough to stay alive, Nemo made a second pivot.

He boosted the efforts of a small, eccentric group called the Philosopher Kings. They had been campaigning against the Panopticon since its inception. In Utopia Five, the Kings' founder received a windfall and some well-timed advice from a mysterious benefactor. In the nuclear aftermath, Wigborough Wick persuaded the shocked populace to turn off the all-seeing-eye and concentrate on feeding themselves. The pivot was complete: "Utopia Five: The Unwatched Masses".

# CHALLENGE

*Analog 2053*

"A world with no Panopticon!" my brother leapt in. "It was a challenge. You know we can't change anything before the Panopticon went live? So, I couldn't assassinate the inventor, or some politician, like normal. I had to get everyone to *choose* to turn off the Eye. That's how I met Wigborough."

Nemo was speaking excitedly to Kirby. "Wigborough had already spent years thinking about it. We knew it'd be hard to persuade people to decommission the drones after they'd been so critical in the Summer, but I couldn't turn the

Panopticon off *before* '36 because civilization would fry."

"Dystopia Seven: We're All Toast!" I interjected.

"Yes. I'd tried that before," continued Nemo. "So, I only had one option. I'd have to stop the Hot Summer from happening."

"Would that have been possible?" asked Kirby, frustratingly slowly. "According to your game rules, you can only change things back to 2025. That's only 11 years to work with."

"I reckoned it could be done with a bit of geo-engineering." Nemo continued, "I'd have to dim the world for a decade. Have you heard of Krakatoa?"

Kirby nodded.

"The eruption threw enough crap into the atmosphere to shade the planet for years. I needed something ten times that size, so I nuked Southeast Asia and convinced the game engine it would have been enough to avoid the meltdown in '36."

"So, you're saying the Hot Summer could have been avoided? All those people could have been saved?" Kirby looked shaken.

"Yes and no." Nemo went on, "I just put the Summer back a few decades. Loads of people still died from starvation and the explosion. But it worked. During the harvest failures the Panopticon seemed like a distraction. It was relatively easy to get it switched off."

He paused. "I liked Wigborough, so as a surprise I got his denizen to pull the plug. All I had to do was bung him some campaign cash in the sim, give him my excellent marketing advice, and the Panopticon was history." Nemo looked around for appreciation.

"Were you supposed to be building a Utopia or a Dystopia?" I asked, coldly.

"Er, actually I didn't know. That was the point. It was an experiment to find out what the world might be like with no all-seeing-eye. Originally, I wasn't even going to publish it. I only did it for me and you." He looked at me. "We'd been arguing about the Panopticon for years."

I was worried.   I could see they weren't convinced Wick was dangerous.  My exploding flat seemed inexplicable.

"But you decided to show what you had created to Wigborough?" I said.

Nemo nodded hesitantly.   "Yes, I gave him a login.  I thought he'd like it.  But after he saw it, he went all weird.  Then a few days ago we met in the pub, and he said he wanted us to visit Angelsea and meet you here.   I'd got a car stashed for emergencies, so I agreed."

"We've been waiting for you to show up.  I knew you'd come and find me."   My brother looked baffled.  "It was only a game!  Why on earth should Wigborough start murdering people?"

I shook my head.  "The Panopticon has been an obsession of Wick's for a long time.  He thinks it changed people in ways they didn't choose, and I suspect he felt guilty he'd failed to stop it happening.  When you turned up with Utopia Five, it was too much to handle."

"Virtual reality is really convincing if you aren't used to it," I continued, "And Wick wasn't.  You'd just shown him a world where not only had all his dreams come true, he was a hero. In his eyes, he'd saved everyone. I'm going to take a wild guess and say he was inspired to bring that about in reality. The trouble was, he realised Utopia Five was a threat as well as a promise."

"He got a bit obsessed with it and he wasn't as happy as I'd expected," Nemo mused.

"When I played it, it was obvious it wasn't a world I wanted to live in," I said. "We've forgotten crime. Why on earth would we want it back? We can trust everyone we meet now." I looked at Kirby for support.

Cross nodded. "*That* is a utopia."

"I imagine Wick saw what I saw – people wouldn't want to live in Utopia Five." I continued, "And you told him the only other person who'd seen it so far was me?"

Nemo looked stricken.

"So, he thought you and I were about to kill off his vision. Utopia Five is essentially propaganda for the Panopticon and he believed we were about to deliver it to the whole world."

Nemo gave every impression he was about to be sick. Now I just had to convince Kirby.

"In Control, I saw Wick plant a bomb in my flat," I said to Cross, "And then he watched to see when I was online and not paying attention so he could detonate it."

Kirby looked thoughtful. "Half of Wick's problems would be gone. Only Nemo left."

"Actually," I corrected him, "Killing Nemo and I would only take him back to square one. My guess is he's set his sights higher. His goal is to take out the Panopticon and to do that, he has to destroy Deus."

I continued, "Nemo could get him in front of you. Once I'd escaped the bomb, he knew I'd have to come and find my brother. All he had to do was wait until I arrived. He could take all three of us out in one go. Get rid of Utopia Five, Deus and Control." I stared at Kirby. "If he comes back and finds me here, he'll kill us."

Nemo and Kirby looked horrified. Great. I'd finally convinced them to get the hell out of there.

Nemo and I pulled the shocked, elderly men out of their chairs and pushed them towards the door. I was behind Nemo when I realised the two in front had stopped in the corridor and seemed to be shoving their way back in. We'd taken too long. "He's coming!" cried Kirby.

We backed away from the entrance and I looked around. There was nowhere for me to hide. On the positive side, the purpose of my coming here was to confront Wick, not to hang out in a broom cupboard. I had just hoped to get Nemo to safety before our denouement. There was no chance of that now. I stood in the centre of the room and waited for Wick to walk in.

The man who strode through the door and then stopped was both very familiar to me and not at all. Although we'd never met, I'd spent the last 24 hours reviewing every critical moment in the life of the thin, sandy-haired individual in front of me. He was not a bad person. If I'd had a drink with him twelve months before he met my brother, I'd probably have liked him.

He spoke. "Lee Sands. Finally, we meet."

I took a deep breath. According to every sim I'd run, we only had one chance. I had to make this man angry.  Very angry.  I was going to have to be more annoying than I had ever been in my life. That was quite annoying.

"*Finally we meet*?" I replied, scornfully.  "That's a little am-dram, Wigborough.  Been practicing in the mirror?"

"Be quiet!"  He pulled out a nasty-looking handgun and pointed it threateningly at me and the others.

Wick stared at Kirby.  "I assume from your current cowering that Lee told you about my demolition project."  He laughed and then glared at me.  "Now you have finally arrived I can get this finished."

I guessed he was warming up to a speech outlining his plan.  He'd clearly been watching his own sleek denizen too long - he sounded more like the smug version in Utopia Five than his real self of a year ago.  I suspected he was about to tell us how he intended to kill us.

"I can describe my plans to you in complete safety because I'm afraid none of you will leave this room alive.  As soon as..."

"Are you going to shoot us?" I interrupted.

Wick narrowed his eyes in irritation and continued, "As soon as Lee arrived..." He paused dramatically. "Your fates were..."

"You've hidden a bomb in the room?" I enquired.

He continued more loudly, "Your fates were sealed!" He finished quickly and looked at me in triumph.

Now we were going to hear his evil scheme. It would be nice to get my theory confirmed.

"Why?" I asked.

"I, Wigborough Wick, am the head of a secret organization – The Philosopher Kings – that has spent two decades planning how to free humanity from the tyranny of the Panopticon!" He stared at Kirby. "Slowly and surely, we drew our plans against you." He paused while we all looked appreciative of his War of the Worlds reference. It was good to be reminded the fate of the world was in the hands of a bunch of geeks.

"I also refer to my pub quiz team as a secret organization," I said.

Wick barely blinked. His ability to ignore my provocation was admirable, if frustrating. As a teacher, I guess that was his day job.

He continued, "Twenty years ago, my comrade Keith," he waved at the hitherto unnamed accomplice who looked as terrified as everyone else. "Infiltrated Omniscience and ever since, he has been corrupting the feeds, sabotaging Deus, and undermining the bot that is controlling society!"

"Was he? Nemo and I never noticed anything." I commented conversationally. "How about you Kirby?"

Cross looked thoughtful. "Nothing in particular. In fact, Keith has always had exemplary performance reviews." He looked over at him. "I thought you'd just dropped by for our usual cup of tea. It was nice to see you."

Keith assumed the expression of a man who had been unexpectedly complimented by his boss, whilst possibly being held at gunpoint by a lunatic who may or may not be his own accomplice.

"SILENCE!" yelled Wigborough. "Keith was playing the long game! We have always known we would never achieve our aim without destroying Deus and Control by eradicating you three!"

Keith glanced uncomfortably between Kirby and Wick, looking like he had no idea how he'd got into his current situation.

Wick shook his pistol. "That is the key to freedom for humanity! People have been lured away from self-determination by a search algorithm and a nice user interface! You have deprived us of our true destiny! While you exist, the Panopticon will always be there, and people will forever be repressed by the collective will!" He had reached a screeching crescendo by this point. "Our destiny..."

"Yes, but," I started.

"STOP INTERRUPTING ME!" shouted Wick, raised his gun and took a step towards me.

The next 0.48 seconds were almost as much of a surprise to me as they were to him. Before I had time to think, Wick was falling to the ground, knocked unconscious by a single punch to the jaw and I was holding his weapon.

"Bloody hell," said Nemo. "How did you do that?"

"Code." I replied. "You should try it."

# ESCAPE

*Analog 2036*

Nemo shook me awake. "We have to go," he said. "Now!"

I jumped out of bed and shoved my feet into trainers. At Deus' recommendation, Nemo and I had been sleeping in our clothes for weeks.

"Are Mum and Dad back?" I asked as we tore through the front door and onto the street.

Outside, the wind had changed direction. It was blowing strong and frighteningly hot. The night sky was glowing a dark orange.

My brother shook his head. "They're still at the town meeting. Deus says we can't wait." He got the glazed look that meant he was listening to his earpiece. "It says we have to head northeast to the sea marsh." He went pale. "It's five miles. Deus says we need to make it there in seventeen minutes." He stared at me. "I don't know what to do. Should we find Dad?"

I looked at Nemo's face. Deus was never wrong.

"Get the bikes."

I ran back into the house. I reckoned we had to leave inside 30 seconds to meet the deadline.

In the hall, I grabbed a bugout bag. I'd put a couple together months earlier. I left one for our parents, snatched up my phone, and considered whether we had time for a conversation.

"Deus! Tell Mum and Dad where we've gone," I whispered, then I shouted at my brother, "We're going where we're told – the sea. You lead."

The next minutes were a blur of frantic cycling in the ominous light. The bot directed us along whatever clear roads there were. We detoured across fields of dry grass. A few times we seemed to be riding straight at the flames and only passed in front by a few feet.

Deus picked routes that kept us clear of smoke as well as the fire. I had oxygen masks in my rucksack, but we never have had time to put them on.

When we got to the edge of the marsh, we could see fire following us. It had reached the other side of the field we were in. Ahead, the tide was out. A mile of grass hummocks threaded with channels of thick mud stood between us and the water. I pulled a torch out of my bag, and we abandoned the bikes. They wouldn't help us now.

The marsh wouldn't burn, but it was like the nightmare of some gothic writer. It was a labyrinth of banks, deep mud, and quicksand. Ready to trap us at any misstep. We'd have to jump from mound to mound in the dark, hoping we'd find a route we could follow through it before the tide returned. There was a beach on the other side where we should be safe, but how could we possibly get there?

I switched the torch on and looked at my little brother. In front, it was pitch black. Behind, the smoke was rolling towards us. No matter what, we had to move.

As I gingerly stepped forward, a light materialized in the darkness a hundred feet ahead. We froze while it slowly bobbed closer until I could finally make it out.

"I asked Deus for help," said Nemo.

Luckily for us, we didn't live in a Victorian novel.

Some quadcopters were too small for firefighting but could still handle GPS and satellite maps. A guide drone's steady glow illuminated 10 feet around itself to lead you in smoke or darkness. This one could take us through the maze.

Two hours after our rescuer had appeared, we stumbled, exhausted, onto the shingle spit at the far side of the marsh. We'd had to stop and put oxygen masks on almost immediately. Even so, Nemo was still coughing from the smoke.

We were both covered in thick mud. I'd fallen in once and just managed to claw my way out. We collapsed onto the stones and looked back for the first time. We couldn't see anything but flames.

The sun rose and, eventually, the coast guard picked us up. That didn't happen until nearly the evening. The guide drone had reported we were uninjured and had food and water from my rucksack. We were relatively safe. Not a high priority.

The authorities didn't take us back home. There was nothing left there. Not of our house or our town. A freak change in the wind had swept a wall of fire 10 miles across from the south to the sea.

A handful of survivors struggled into the rescue centres over the next 24 hours. They didn't include our parents.

# TRUMP SUIT

## *Analog 2053*

Ten minutes after I'd knocked Wick unconscious, we'd handcuffed him with the plastic ties I'd brought and dragged him back to the lift.

I suspected there was a bomb of some kind hidden in Kirby's suite, but we'd find someone more expert to locate that. I had a feeling that when Wick woke up, he'd tell us all about it. He clearly liked the sound of his own voice these days.

The elevator reached the ground floor of the northwest tower. We'd entered the underground complex less than an hour before. It felt longer. Now, the sun was rising, and we were greeted not by empty corridors, but an army of technicians setting up chairs, tables, and equipment. I recognized a few people from the camp.

A doctor sprinted over. He was a cheerfully plump guy in his twenties who I'd drunk a pint with the night before. He gave Wick a brief checkup.

"So, this is your nemesis, eh?" He gave me a wink. "He seems harmless enough. He's just coming round. I'll go and find some help and we can get him into the ambulance."

As the medic dived off again Keith said, "I'll go with Wigborough." He sighed. "He's really alright, you know. He just got a bit carried away. He always complained we were living in a gaol. Now I guess that's where he'll end up."

"Ooh, ironic," said Nemo. I kicked him in the shin. This whole mess was his fault.

Ray and Laura walked into the tower from the tree-filled ward. "What a lovely place this is!" exclaimed Laura.

Ray joined me in gazing down at Wick. "Well, that fella will be popular in prison."

I raised my eyebrows.

"Their adult education programme is chronically short of maths teachers," explained Laura, "They are hardly ever incarcerated. I understand they are already looking forward to seeing him."

The rest of the day was spent tracking down and fixing the havoc wreaked by Wigborough Wick and his penchant for explosive materials. Catterwade used one of her smaller remote drones to locate the bomb in Kirby's offices and help Omniscience's explosives people to defuse it. Ray informed me quietly that Catterwade had been in the army until the Summer. That didn't surprise me. The forces had had a traumatic time in '36.

That evening Nemo, Kirby and I joined the rest of the caravan group for dinner. Omniscience had set up a refectory amongst the trees in the ward to feed the workers. Ray, Laura, and others were all camping outside the castle that night.

"The world isn't ready to live without the Panopticon," said Kirby. "Maybe if we had ten years to prepare, we could do it, but society is still too fragile right now. Losing Deus and Control would have destroyed everything. Wick was mad!

Worse, he was a fool. Even if individualism were the future of humanity, we can't do it yet. Deus knows I've thought about it. We'd pay with complete collapse."

I picked up my glass and swirled the beer around. "In Utopia Five, Wigborough Wick was a rich famous big shot. He'd reshaped the world to reflect his beliefs. Nemo gave him access to the game and, according to the logs, he spent hours watching his denizen on TV giving theatrical speeches about how much better everything was because of him. Utopia Five made fame, power, and influence feel real for him. It was like something he already had. But it wasn't true. Maybe it's not surprising he couldn't handle it. Who could?"

Nemo hadn't been able to resist showing Wick his creation: Utopia Five. My bet was that changed the man. The game made all his desires a reality. After all, that's what sims are for. Utopia Five let Wick see the prize and imagine he had already won it. It made it all real and him willing to kill to keep it.

"Save me from an enemy with something to gain or a friend with something to lose," said Laura. "It's very sad. Before he met Nemo, he was rather a pleasant man. I have recommended he receive a psychiatric judgement rather than a criminal one."

I frowned in agreement. My brother had a lot to answer for.

Handing round fresh beers, Ray explained their sudden arrival that morning. "The whole camp decided to follow you. When we got here the place was deserted. We assumed you were handling Wick." Ray nodded at me. "So, we came in to wait."

Nemo had been uncharacteristically subdued all afternoon. I think Laura had had a long conversation with him about his role in events.

"What I want to know," he said to me directly, "Was how *did* you handle Wick? That was like a ninja superpower. You couldn't do that when I left." He paused. "And don't say you found a really good karate class."

I gave him a withering look. "You're losing it Nemo. That was what we do for a living. You're obviously spending too much time picking kitchen surfaces out of home magazines."

Laura cleared her throat. Earlier that evening they'd all watched the recording of my very brief fight with Wick. "Actually Lee, I think we'd all be interested to hear how you did that. Was it luck?"

"Luck isn't a thing," I replied, and spent the next hour explaining.

As I've mentioned before, the Nautilus games engine isn't an oracle.

That's why we can't just bet big on a horse race and retire. The worlds it creates, like Utopia Five, are not predictions. Nautilus can't see the future because a few seconds after even a simple event there are hundreds of thousands of possible outcomes. A few seconds later, millions. Then billions. Nautilus can tell you what could happen. It can't tell you which single thing will.

However, over a tiny stretch of time, in limited circumstances, and from very specific initial conditions Nautilus can narrow the possibilities down. Those aren't the kind of odds I'd bet my life on. Usually.

When I create a new world, I start with the Control sim, which is basically reality. Then I change something and roll the sim forward to see how the change might play out. I find out what the cumulative effect would be. That's all everyone thinks Nautilus is, but that's just the start.

Tiny alterations lead to completely different results. Making a pivot happen a fraction of a second earlier or later can generate completely distinct worlds. My secret is, I can instruct Nautilus to make millions of tweaks to a pivot, look through the legion of potential outcomes, and pick the best. It can review every possible consequence and give me the world I want.

"The Nautilus behaviour engine knew everything the Panopticon did about Wigborough Wick," I told the group. "That included every weapon he'd run across in 28 years."

"It's quite hard to get hold of a gun now." I looked at Ray for confirmation and he nodded. "That pistol Wick was waving around," I continued, "must have been left over from the hothead youth he talked about. Nautilus estimated with overwhelming probability it was his only weapon."

"I'd had no idea he even had a gun," said Nemo.

I went on, "The copy of Nautilus running on my suit had nearly thirty years of recordings of Wick. Once I'd finally downloaded the last four days from our machines at the Heavenly Host, his denizen was mine."

"Yesterday, I ran over a million simulated hand-to-hand and armed sub-second encounters with Wigborough Wick using his Control denizen. I covered every possible reaction, movement, and countermovement."

I paused. "I simulated fights with his gun and every other knife, candlestick, or potentially dangerous object he might have got his hands on. That generated 98,537 possible futures. In 84,678 of them Lee Sands died in the battle."

"Bloody hell!" said Ray. "So, you only had a, what, fifteen percent chance of survival? That's bad odds. You should never have gone in."

"Agreed. That's why Lee Sands didn't fight Wigborough Wick. I'm not a hand-to-hand combat expert. No karate class would be enough to fix that." I grinned at Nemo.

"So, who did fight him?" he asked.

I looked down at the attire that had served me well since carrying me out of an exploding building a few days before.

I'd never understood why people spent their billions on a house or a fairy tale castle or even a moon base. It was so unimaginative. My black suit was a lot less flashy but, anyway, it's tacky to show off.

I'd read in the early days of tech, billionaire founders liked to wear an identical outfit every day. I felt the same. When I got up, I preferred to already be dressed in a Mars and military-grade, vacuum-rated, programmable servo-assisted power exoskeleton.

I'd upgraded mine with state-of-the-art computational hardware and sensors. All connected with a superconducting internal network. I liked to be prepared. Oh, and it was a haptic stillsuit. You mustn't forget the basics. Optimized for high-speed computation and fast physical response, I called it my edge.

In a single place, for a single person, and for a very short period of time, Nautilus could effectively narrow the future of a brief encounter to less than 100,000 possibilities. In the test run simulations with Wick, my suit had proved capable of detecting and handling all of them.

I knew my best chance to get everyone out was to stay alive until Wigborough Wick triggered one of the initial conditions I'd simulated. That meant him being within arm's reach of me with his hands visible. I'd reckoned I needed to bait a lunatic with a gun until he tried to punch me. It worked. Eventually.

As soon as he stepped into range, the suit took over. *I* didn't have a superconducting internal network, so the whole thing was over before I'd even realized it had started.

# CHEATING

*Analog 2053*

"You used your supersuit?" said Nemo, when I'd finished. "That's basically cheating."

"I got you one for Christmas," I retorted. "It's not my fault you never wear it."

"So, everything's back to normal." My brother grinned. "Cheers to that." He opened a beer.

"Actually, I have a question." Laura turned to look at my brother. "Why on earth did you build a tool that could deceive the Panopticon? Could that not still destroy society by dismantling our faith in the eye?"

"Oh yes, I was tinkering with that to hide my browsing history from Lee," Nemo replied. "It worked great too, but as soon as I realised I could fool the Panopticon I went to Kirby."

Kirby nodded and Nemo continued, "That was nearly a year ago. I thought if I could hoodwink the eye, eventually other people would too. We released my code on the greynet six months ago. Don't panic! It's perfectly safe. Kirby found a flaw. He patched the OmniscientView to recognise it and silently flag it up. We can tell if data is faked. We reckoned it was better to have bad guys using my algorithm than writing their own and maybe finding one that actually worked."

"What is the flaw?" I asked.

Nemo and Kirby smirked at one another. "We wouldn't want to *delay* you by explaining," said Nemo and they both sniggered.

OK, now I had another annoying person in my life. Great.

"The only thing I don't understand," I said, "Was why the Panopticon sent Laura and Ray up here to handle some kind of data problem days ago, when Nemo only started screwing with the network to get my attention yesterday."

"Ah," said Ray, "I'm afraid we told you a bit of a lie." He looked at Laura.

"It was not a coincidence Ray and I joined your journey here," Laura said apologetically. "After the explosion, the Panopticon sent us to keep an eye on you."

She continued, "You must realise, you and Nemo are important people. Control going offline caused havoc. It may not be the most common way to access the Panopticon, but as you are aware there are things Control can do that Deus and the direct feeds cannot. Control may have started as a game but now it is critical infrastructure."

I nodded. I'd restored the systems as soon as Nemo gave me back my access.

"The Panopticon assemblies are worried Control is too vital to remain in the hands of only two young people," Laura said and nodded at my brother and me. "The same is true of Kirby and Deus." She looked at him. "Even you won't live forever."

Kirby looked shifty. "I could be around a lot longer; Gates must be ancient. No one ever comments on that."

Laura ignored him. "You three, Deus, and Control were nearly wiped out today by a rogue schoolteacher. We need to do something about that."

"Yeah," said Ray. "Wigborough Wick is not the only madman in the world. Most of them may be less lucky, but a lot will be better funded and a great deal more competent. Being single points of failure is what made you targets."

I thought for a moment. Kirby had to retire sometime, and Nemo was right, I did work all the time. Running Nautilus didn't leave much room for anything else. Oddly, the last week had been a nice break, even with a maniac bomber on my tail. Maybe the three of us did need to rethink.

"Why don't you both stay here for a while?" Kirby said. "Lee, you literally don't have a home to go back to and Nemo is always welcome to visit." He paused. "As long as he doesn't bring a friend next time. I have some interesting ideas for Control we could look at. We have guest rooms in the castle."

Nemo and I looked at one another. Maybe this could be fun.

# EPILOGUE

## Control 1963

Back on the grassy knoll, I watched the

approaching motorcade.

"If these denizens were sentient, what would our responsibilities be?" I mused. "Should we leave them alone to forge their own destiny or interfere to make it nicer for them? Should they be allowed to choose the behaviour of their deity not just their own behaviour? Would their collective behaviour trump their god's anyway?"

I went on, "It's hard to change things to the way you want, even with god-like powers, and we should know - sims wriggle out of our control just from simple randomness. I can hardly imagine how hard it would be with conscious denizens."

Nemo always got bored when I got introspective. He yawned. "I think that whole Wigborough denouement was a bit 'Mary Sue'," he said. "You were implausibly good at everything. Especially the suit stuff. You're going to have to tone that down or people will think you're a dick."

I looked at my brother. "I'm the third richest person on the planet." I decided Nemo was going to have to suck up some more introspection. "In every world, especially the real one, money is a bloody superpower. I've spent ten years learning how to use it to get the results I want. If I wasn't a Mary Sue, then what the hell would I be playing at?" I demanded.

"You may have a point about the money," he conceded.

"I still haven't forgiven you for the lockout," I said.

"It's good for you to occasionally speak to some humans. I don't know what you're moaning about. You left the house and found an army. I made friends with one person, and he turned out to be a psychopath who tried to kill me."

"That was just bad luck," I protested. Except I knew Wick wasn't a psychopath when Nemo met him, just a grumpy teacher with a minor hobby in sedition. I decided not to mention that.

"Are our parents still alive in Utopia Five?" I suddenly asked.

"Yes, but don't go and see them. With so little data to work from, their avatars are just shadows. Visiting will only make you think worse of them. It wouldn't be fair."

My little brother was annoying, but he was probably right. So, I suspected, was Laura. She'd told me Nemo and I had too much money and way too much concentrated power. I agreed. Nautilus couldn't only be us any longer.

The good news was, we could keep an eye on Control and the games from anywhere. Nemo and I would stay at Angelsea for a while and work with Laura and Ray to learn how the Panopticon and WorldGov managed things. We wanted to collaborate on a couple of projects with Kirby too. He had lots of ideas for how Control could use his feeds better and his Omniscience folk could help us look after Nautilus. Maybe I could even go on holiday occasionally.

WorldGov wanted me to build some Utopias that might point them in a better direction for the other planets. Utopia Five woke them up to some of Nautilus's possibilities and they'd like us to look at how society might work on Mars and the Moon.

I also wanted to handle Laura to avoid Control getting nationalized. If Nemo and I screwed up again like we did last week it would be.

I clearly needed to pay more attention to what my brother was up to. I trusted Nemo, but he was an idiot sometimes and a terrifyingly clever one. I reckoned I'd need to watch him a lot more closely than I had been. Perhaps I could get Kirby to help. Although, I was already worried Nemo might be a bad influence on Cross.

I had a lot to do.

# TIMELINE

**2025** – 8th January 2025 is Full Transparency Day.  The day the Panopticon is turned on.

**2030** – Deus1 launched.

**'30-'35** The Panopticon is gradually rolled out worldwide accompanied by a reduction in crime, more informed debate, better political engagement, and higher productivity.  Deus builds on its lead and becomes the most widely used and trusted application in the world.

**2036** – The Hot Summer: fires, floods, ice storms, and tornados engulf the globe.  Over one billion are killed.  Mass exoduses occur from many land masses and areas.  The refugee population surges.

**2037** – WorldGov and the Panopticon Assemblies are formed.

**2037** – Stillsuits invented.

**2038** – The Quantum Leap occurs – vastly improved image processing and storage using quantum technology.

**2042** – Nautilus 1: Sauron's Eye. The first full world–sim based on Panopticon data is launched (will become Control).

**2043** – Dystopia 1 launched.

**2050** – DeusX launched.

**2053** – Utopia Five

**Conundra, the next in the Panopticon series, is out now…**

# CHAPTER 1 - ARRIVAL

*Conundra, September 2054*

Night had already fallen when I stepped off the train and onto Conundra station. I pulled out a paper map and tried to flick down my suit visor to magnify it before remembering I had no suit here. This was a tech-free city. At least, for visitors.

The platform was busy. Several hundred people had just disembarked and were standing and staring at the place. It looked like a scene from a 1940's war movie, if every evacuee had just arrived from some random point in history. I glanced at the map, which told me I was in the Nostalgia zone. That wasn't my period. I was planning to walk to the Victorian era.

I was glad Nemo had picked an industrial age for my hotel - at least I could wear vaguely normal clothes there. Even so, I'd had to submit my wardrobe to the verisimilitude committee. I glanced down at my outfit: black trousers, white shirt, black leather coat and goggles. *It's not a neoprene suit,* I thought, *but you can't have everything.*

Surrounding me was a group of Roman senators, wrestling with wheelie-suitcases. A porter appeared and quietly relieved them of their anachronistic luggage. I guessed he'd deliver it to their hotel rooms. In private, they could be as out-of-character as they wanted but in public, themes clearly had to be maintained.

Looking about, I reckoned most of the milling visitors were Romans. A toga would have been a much better costume for a sweltering September. *Damn*, I thought.

On the platform, a few others were as overdressed as me. A dozen men wearing trench coats and wide brimmed hats were loitering around with their collars up, smoking cigarettes. I wondered if there was a convention of private detectives in the city – or of retro flashers. Hopefully crime was all they were there to expose. I wasn't intending to stay long enough in the Nostalgia zone to find out.

I picked up my battered leather suitcase and looked around carefully. The crowd had quickly thinned out as the guests presumably headed to their hotels. I was in no rush. I knew that officially your Conundra storyline didn't start until you'd arrived at your lodgings and got settled in. *If this was my game*, I thought, *I'd say the same thing, then stick a clue in the first five minutes. See who was paying attention.* I turned slowly in a circle, observing everything going on. I was looking for something that seemed wrong. Was there anything out of place?

I watched the train pull away. It left the few remaining new arrivals alone with city residents playing railway workers, guides, or any other part that might be required for the storylines. I gazed across their faces, seeing expressions that were bemused, excited, bored, keen, horrified, tired.

*Horrified.* I swivelled back to a figure on the far side of the station, close to the other end of the platform. That was what I was looking for. Horror wasn't one of the emotions I would normally expect from a holidaymaker. Although, I didn't go on holiday that often. Perhaps my expectations were unrealistically high.

A young woman had been looking back over her shoulder with an exaggerated expression of fear. She turned her head and hurried towards the station exit. I decided to follow, pushing my way through a crowd of white-robed Romans that had materialised between us. My eyes stayed locked on my target, and I tried not to tread on anyone's sandals with my steel-capped boots. *This is one of the many problems with mixing your genres*, I thought. I always tried to avoid it myself.

The person I was attempting to tail had a cloud of brown hair half-tucked under a headscarf and was wearing a long raincoat that covered her clothing. It was a patent, and poor, attempt at a disguise - she was clearly being deliberately easy to spot.

It suddenly occurred to me I could be muscling in on someone else's story. I looked around and decided I didn't think so. She wasn't dressed as a Roman and none of the other new visitors seemed to be following her - the only people moving around purposefully on the platform were centurions. I reckoned they looked more like security guards than other guests. *Anyway*, I thought, *if I'm intruding on the wrong plotline the Conundra systems will untangle it.* That must happen all the time.

I moved carefully through the throng towards the woman. She stopped every few minutes and looked behind her in terror. I didn't think she had spotted me yet. *Her act is a bit overdone*, I thought, *but I'll go with it.* This was a rather obvious plot kick-off but I'd seen worse. I shrugged, if I was being honest, I'd written worse.

I emerged from the crowd just as she disappeared out of the station into the unlit streets outside. Still carrying my suitcase, I ran after her, bursting through the double doors in time to see her vanish into an alleyway. That clinched it. So far, so stereotyped. I was supposed to infer from her terror she was a lone woman being pursued by an enemy. It was a classic trope. Of course, in real life no one being chased by a villain would dash into a dark dead-end. *You'd have to be an idiot*, I thought, as I sprinted in behind her.

The passageway was narrow, and it was almost pitch black in there. I cursed the Victorians for their lack of IR scopes, pulled a box of matches out of my pocket, and lit one. I saw the woman had reached a brick end wall and turned in seemingly genuine panic. She was actually good, I thought – wasted in this clichéd part.

"Who are you?" she whispered, hoarsely.

"A friend." I replied. That was generally the magic key phrase, even though words are cheap and, in reality, I could have been about to punch her out and nick her handbag.

"Please help me!" she cried. "It's all a lie! They're killing people! We have to stop them!"

"I'll do everything I can," I said, getting into the swing of it. "What are these evildoers called and where can I find them?"

"The castle! We have to tell the Warlock before it's too late! We can't trust anyone else!"

The young woman ran back towards me and was still about four feet away when a sharp crack rang out. She theatrically grasped her chest and fell hard onto her knees. *Ouch*, I thought, *I hope they're well-padded under that costume.*

"Leviathan!" she croaked. "Run!"

At that moment, another bullet hit the wall about a foot from me. *That's cutting it close,* I thought, *but I can take a hint.* Recognising my cue to scarper, I ran out of the passage and back onto the street. I took off at speed in the direction of my hotel.

At the end of the road, I stopped and looked back just in time to see a dark figure wearing a distinctive homburg hat slip back into the station.

# To read on, get Conundra by AE Currie from Amazon.

Printed in Great Britain
by Amazon